Ebook ISBN: 978-1-956335-32-3

Paperback ISBN: 978-1-956335-33-0

Audiobook ISBN: 978-1-956335-34-7

Ebook and paperback cover design by Molly Burton at Cozy Cover Designs.

Chapter header and scene break drawings by Etheric Tales.

Axia map designed by Sarah Waites at The Illustrated Page Design.

First published in 2025 by Ringtail Press.

www.melissajacksonbooks.com

 Formatted with Vellum

# MELISSA ERIN JACKSON

# Summary

*Don't look a gift newt in the mouth.*

Deandra has officially moved to Axia! She's rooming with her best friend and cousin, Wendy, and has her trusty baby dragon, Havoc, by her side. She's basking in the joy of having no schedule and no demands on her time. While taking a relaxing stroll with Havoc in Oracle Park one day, however, her peace is shattered when she overhears a violent altercation.

Yet, when she and Havoc track down the source of the commotion, it's not a crime in progress they stumble on, but Chester and his yappy dog, Charles Barksley, squaring off against Deandra's nemesis: Sunshine the fire newt.

After rescuing the pair from Sunshine, Deandra is flabbergasted when, instead of being met with animosity, the newt gives Deandra a gift. The newly acquired coin is grimy, old, and possesses strange magical properties. Deandra is confounded further still when her research into the coin's origins reveals a past not only connected to the fae realm—but to Havoc.

# Reading Order

- **Book 1**: A Mythical Case of Arson
- **Book 1.5**: A Mythical Discovery
- **Book 2**: A Mythical Case of Murder
- **Book 3**: A Mythical Case of Theft
- **Book 4**: A Mythical Case of Homicide
- **Book 5**: A Mythical Case of Kidnapping

Corly Land
Management
Hau
No
Larg
& W
Wheeler Ave
Coterie Road
Heather's
Elixirs
Eddy Way
Telepost
Welcome
Center
Pizza
Place
McClaren
McClaren
McClaren
Grenal Way
AXIA
Axia

Mythic Pet Kitchen
In Flux We Trust
Purl Way
Drug Store
Burned Building
Art Gallery
Cottage
Caddel's Office
Dumpling Hut
Hogarth's Hoagies
Grocery Store
Zombie Cactus
Telepad Station
Unusual Claims
Police Station
POLICE
Extra Sensory Pastry
Oracle Park
Grandparents' House

Deandra walked along the path that circled Oracle Park, her dragon happily trotting ahead of her. It was the middle of the afternoon and she, blissfully, had nowhere to be. There wasn't a sense of dread in her belly over the reality that her day was to be spent making expensive coffees for ungrateful customers. She didn't need to check her bank account and log the week's figures in a spreadsheet, doing the math on how many ride-share gigs she'd need to do to guarantee she could make rent this month.

When Havoc stopped to sniff a rose, she halted on the path and tipped her head back, basking in the warm sunlight on her skin.

It was a truly beautiful day. The sky was a cloudless blue. The faint sound of laughing children on the playground was punctuated by the occasional soft quack of a duck paddling in the nearby pond.

This was all somewhat dampened by old Chester's frantic shouting, and his dog, Charles Barksley, yipping his little head off from somewhere up ahead. She instantly knew it was him. Despite being a new resident of Axia, she'd already grown accustomed to Chester yelling at someone or something while walking his constantly barking dog.

*"Get away from us, you monster! Get away! Help!"* came Chester's distant voice.

Deandra glanced down at Havoc, who was sitting on his haunches and closely watching a bee. Hopefully he wouldn't try to snatch the thing out of the air—he'd tried and missed several times during their walk already, despite Deandra admonishing him. Though, if Havoc got stung and his face swelled up, it would not only teach him a lesson, but it would be an excuse for Deandra to see Dr. Cruz Caddel.

She was fairly certain the ball was in her court when it came to seeing the veterinarian again. A simple text message would no doubt work, so using her pet's potential self-inflicted injury as a means to see him was admittedly a touch extreme.

Dr. Caddel was one of the few people in town who knew Havoc was actually a dragon and not a dire wolf. The enchanted white leather collar Havoc wore shielded his true identity from the population at large. It was Dr. Caddel's theory that only people Havoc trusted, and thereby looped into his inner circle, saw him for what he truly was.

That circle was more of a dot, though, as Deandra was currently the only person on the list of trusted pod members.

She and Dr. Caddel had texted quite a few times back when Havoc was still in animal jail after being seized by Ranger Vicks and Ranger Dancy of Parks Management. Dr. Caddel had offered to swing by the facility to drop off Havoc's cold medicine and to make sure he was okay. And, even more importantly, to assure his glamouring collar was still around his neck. Dr. Caddel had also been cooking up a way to break Havoc—albeit through legal means—out of confinement.

**Deandra**
Officer Dancy said he'll be checking on him tomorrow. He seems like a good guy. He might be able to help you with whatever your mysterious prison break plan is

**Cruz**
Noted

**Deandra**
I appreciate you doing this. Do I owe you anything? Medicine delivery probably isn't in your job description …

**Cruz**
Buy me lunch sometime and we'll call it even.

Had he meant that as a date? Was it a platonic suggestion? Was it a throwaway offer since, at that time, Deandra hadn't made a decision about moving to Axia? Dr. Caddel had probably thought he'd never see her again.

*"Help! Charles Barksley, stop! You'll lose an eye!"*

Deandra glanced in the direction of the shouting elderly man and his yappy dog but couldn't see them from here. Surely someone *else* would come to Chester's aid. Right? If Deandra strolled up with Havoc in tow, it would set off Chester even more.

Last month, Chester had made it abundantly clear he thought a dire wolf was too dangerous for anyone to keep as a pet. Actually, he didn't think dire wolves should be in Axia at all. The last thing she needed was for Chester to wig out on her and call Ranger Vicks.

*"Oh, Goddess above! Won't anyone help us?"*

Groaning, Deandra glanced down at Havoc. "Let's go see what that's about. Try not to scare the crap out of Charles Barksley, okay?"

Havoc offered a chirp, but his muzzle was bunched as he did it, muddying an already unclear message.

They set off toward the commotion. Deandra kept hoping that whatever the apparent threat was would be dealt with before she reached Chester. His dog hadn't stopped barking in several minutes, though that didn't mean much. A niggling fear voiced the possibility that Chester could be in the midst of getting mugged, and Charles Barksley was attempting to play hero, protecting his human.

Deandra picked up the pace.

By the time they rounded the bend in the walking path, Deandra could finally see Chester and his dog. There was no mugger in sight. In fact, there were no people around at all. Charles Barksley was squared up against a bush covered in small red berries, and he was barking and snarling at it as if it were a fearsome monster, not an immobile bit of shrubbery. The dog lunged with enough force that Chester had to grab hold of the leash with both hands to keep from losing hold of it. The dog couldn't have weighed more than ten pounds, though; Chester acted as if he were fighting against the might of a ravenous tiger.

Deandra made eye contact with a woman at the far end of the path who, upon seeing Charles Barksley losing his ever-loving mind, came to a dead stop. She offered Deandra a tentative wave.

Chester yelped as his tennis shoes slid half an inch forward on the dirt path. "Charles Barksley! Stop this instant! You're too brave for your own good. Oh, Goddess, help us!"

The watching woman winced dramatically and shook her head

in a clear sign of "Nope, not today!" She made an abrupt about-face, then headed back the other way.

*Coward.*

"Hi, Chester!" Deandra called from several feet away, raising her voice to be heard over the dog's increasingly high-pitched barks. She stopped in the middle of the path so as to not freak the pair out further. "What's the problem?"

Chester glanced over. His eyes widened when they landed on her, then grew wider still when he spotted Havoc.

He went rigid—then screamed bloody murder.

*Oh, for goodness' sake ...*

"You stay right there, young lady! It was within my rights to call Parks Management about your hellhound! Even if he wasn't the one who committed the arson, he's still a danger! You weren't complying with the leash laws. You can't seek your revenge on me now in retaliation! Help! *Heeeelp!*"

Charles Barksley had been distracted from his war with the bushes by all the shouting. He stood in the middle of the path now, too, facing Deandra and Havoc. He'd gone quiet, which Deandra's ears appreciated.

Havoc had flopped onto his belly when Deandra stopped walking, and his head was wedged between his front paws. He was in the least threatening position possible, save for being on his back. Perhaps that was why Charles Barksley had gone mute, though given the way the small white dog seemed to be trembling, he'd gone quiet out of fear.

"Ranger Vicks was just doing his job," Chester said, also trembling, as if Deandra were the mugger from her own imagined scenario. "And I was doing my job as a concerned citizen. Your ... your dire wolf is a menace. He could tear Charles Barksley's legs off and use them as chew toys."

The dog in question let out a terrified tiny woof.

Havoc lifted his head at the sound of the word "toys."

Chester screamed again. "Please don't hurt us! Your beast was released! You don't have to do this!"

Deandra considered just walking way. Chester was in near hysterics, even though there was a good ten feet separating them. "We just wanted to make sure you were okay. You called for help."

"Not from the likes of *you*!"

Deandra rolled her eyes. "Fine. We're leaving. Have the day you deserve."

Just as she started to turn away, Charles Barksley, with nary a warning, beelined for the bushes again. He moved so quickly, it startled Chester, and the leash was ripped from his hand. The dog dove headlong into the bush, and Chester tipped forward, arms pinwheeling.

Havoc darted forward, dragging Deandra after him. His speed was even more impressive than Charles Barksley's, causing Deandra to lose hold of his leash as well. She stumbled forward but managed not to hit the ground. When she looked up, Havoc was in front of Chester, the dragon standing on his hind legs with his forepaws on the elderly man's chest, propping him up. Chester wasn't necessarily fragile looking, but he couldn't have been younger than eighty—who knew what injuries a hard fall could have caused.

When Chester was steady on his feet again, he scuttled backward a few steps and stared down at Havoc. The man's chest heaved. Havoc's muzzle bunched.

"Come, Havoc," Deandra said.

Without hesitation, Havoc bounded over to her, his leash trailing behind him. When she had the loop firmly in hand, she eyed Chester.

The man wrung his age-spotted hands as his gaze flitted between Deandra and Havoc. "I, uh, thank you."

Deandra only offered a tight nod before she turned away. She'd only made it a few steps when Chester called out.

"Um ... miss?"

She stopped, tipped her head back, and willed herself the patience needed to deal with Chester. When she looked down at Havoc, he offered her a tongue-lolling smile. A laugh slipped out, taking some of her tension with it.

Turning to face Chester once more, she cocked a brow in question.

He was still wringing his hands. He seemed so much older in that moment, as if his overly exuberant dog had been his shield or security blanket and now he was lost without him. The rustling issuing from the bush suggested Charles Barksley was still inside. The barking hadn't resumed, so Deandra was unsure who was winning the fight—foliage or canine.

"Could you possibly help me get Charles Barksley?" Chester asked hesitantly. "An awful fire newt is in there, and I'm worried he's going to get hurt. That newt is nasty—been lunging out of bushes and from branches at us all week. It landed on *me* yesterday and burned a newt-shaped hole in my shirt! It torments Charles Barksley more than any squirrel ever has. What if that terrible thing goes *kaboom* in there while my ... while Charles ... I can't ..."

Deandra held up a hand to quiet him. "I'll see what I can do, okay? I might know the newt."

Chester's thin lips flattened in distaste. "That doesn't surprise me."

Deandra crossed her arms and leveled a flat stare at him.

After several long seconds of silence—save for the rustling in the bushes—Chester caved. "I ... apologize. Charles Barksley was my wife's pride and joy. She passed last year. I can't bear to have anything happen to him."

Dang it.

"Okay. I'm going to unhook Havoc's leash. Don't panic. He won't come anywhere near you, and he won't hurt Charles Barksley, either. But if Havoc is on the other side of the hedge, it might help flush him out," Deandra said.

Chester clearly wanted to say something sassy, but he just wrung his hands and nodded instead.

Deandra unclipped the leash from Havoc's harness. Without her needing to tell him anything, he bounded over to the far side of the bush, partially disappearing from sight. Deandra made her way to the spot where Charles Barksley had been barking when this all started and placed her hands on her knees as she attempted to peer into the thick shrub. She was reminded of doing something similar when she'd dropped by the Clarion pixie clan's residence. Then, she'd had acorns and small bags of lila sugar. If only she had some mealworms with her now.

"Sunshine?" Deandra whisper-hissed. "Sunshine, are you in there?"

The rustling in the bushes stopped for a moment, followed by a startled yelp from a dog. The thrashing within the bush resumed in earnest.

"Sunshine! Leave him alone!" She grabbed a handful of branches with berry-dotted leaves in each hand and pulled them apart. The white of Charles Barksley's fur was easy to spot in the dark depths of the bush, but to get to him, she'd need to get half her torso inside the shrub. The rustling, she realized, was because the dog's leash was tangled around him *and* several branches. She could make out the white of one of the dog's eyes. The poor thing was terrified.

Despite Sunshine having a lot of yellow on her body, the color was only vibrant if her magical stores were topped off. Otherwise, she was mostly black. The newt might have done some terrible things in the past when she was under the magical influence of a forced familiar bond, but regardless of that, there was a calculating intelligence in the amphibian. Not knowing where the psychotic little thing was made Deandra's heart rate double, but she needed to get Charles Barksley out of there. Too much more thrashing, and he could end up seriously hurt.

"You better not bite me," she told the dog, then used her arms to push the branches and leaves out of the way so she could partially wiggle into the bush. The shrub wasn't so deep that she couldn't keep her feet firmly planted on the ground, but the dog was far enough in that, if he'd gotten stuck any deeper, she'd have a much harder time reaching him. Her arms were getting scratched up, but at least there were no thorns to contend with.

Charles Barksley's eyes were wild with fear, and he started bucking and thrashing once he saw Deandra coming for him, but he was so tangled, it was clear he wasn't going anywhere on his own. The fight went out of him once he figured out Deandra was trying to help.

It took some maneuvering and some blind finger flailing to finally unhook his leash from his harness. Deandra looped an arm around the dog as best she could, then slowly pulled him free, leaving the leash in the depths of the bush.

She'd just gotten him out and clipped Havoc's leash to the dog's harness when a blur of black and yellow shot out the top of the bush like a tiny rocket. It landed atop Charles Barksley's head. The dog froze in Deandra's arms for a moment, then scream-howled as if he'd just been electrocuted. Deandra got smacked in the face by a paw, kicked in the stomach by a back leg, and then Sunshine hissed in her face for good measure.

The dog wriggled free, somehow landed on his feet, and then bolted toward Chester. Havoc darted around the bush toward the man, too, presumably to catch him again should he get knocked over. Sunshine was still riding Charles Barksley's head like a hat, hissing in triumph as if she were a cowgirl astride a bucking bull. The leash that trailed after the dog, who was running circles around Chester in blind terror, wrapped around the man's ankles.

Deandra was yelling at Sunshine to knock it off. Chester was yelling at Deandra to "do something!" Havoc chased after Charles Barksley, circling the elderly man again and again as if Chester were a maypole. The poor dog continuously shrieked in fear, though it was hard to tell if he was more scared of Havoc behind him or Sunshine on his head.

A few seconds of sheer pandemonium later, Deandra managed to grab the leash loop, abruptly halting the dog's frantic running. Hitting the brakes dislodged Sunshine. Havoc took off after the newt and quickly grabbed her by the tail with his mouth.

The newt's tail thankfully didn't detach like it did on many mundane lizards and amphibians. Instead, being hung upside-down seemed to trigger something in the newt that made her pass out. She hung limply from Havoc's mouth. If it wasn't for the slight twitch of Sunshine's front feet and the faint pulsing from her soft-yellow spots, Deandra would have thought the newt hadn't survived the chaos.

Once she was sure the immediate threat of Charles Barksley's demise via lunatic newt had passed, Deandra turned to Chester and his dog. "You two okay?"

Chester's eyes were wide. "Seems like it. I think Charles Barksley tinkled on my shoes."

"I think I tinkled on my *own* shoes."

Chester barked a laugh. "Thank you for your help. Maybe we should stay out of the park for a while. That newt has it out for us!"

Deandra wasn't sure if Sunshine had it out for them specifically or the world at large, but she agreed with him all the same. She didn't want to have to call Parks Management on the newt, but launching out of trees at people and tormenting dogs wasn't good for anyone. If Deandra couldn't convince the unhinged newt to find a better hobby, maybe Deandra could contact Ranger Dancy directly to get his advice. "You probably should get out of here before she wakes up. You can keep the leash. Yours might belong to the shrub now."

Chester nodded tightly. "Thanks for the help. And ... uh, I'm sorry for how I treated you before. How I treated *both* of you."

Deandra offered him a small smile, not wanting to tell the man his behavior was okay or forgiven but accepting his apology anyway. Havoc let out a muted chirp without dropping the unconscious newt.

With that, man and canine hustled away.

Blowing out a long breath, Deandra turned toward her dragon and the newt. Figuring the crazed amphibian would wake up as soon as it was no longer upside-down, she told Havoc, "If it looks like Sunshine is going to detonate, jump in to save me, okay?"

The dragon's head sharply ticked to the side, sending Sunshine swaying like a scaly pendulum. His expression seemed to say, *"And how am I supposed to accomplish* that?"

Before she could convince herself not to, she reached out, wrapped her hand around Sunshine's middle, and told Havoc to let her go. He did so, but he clearly had some misgivings.

Holding the newt in her fist, she brought her hand to her eyeline. Sunshine woke up a couple of seconds later, her cold little front feet resting on the side of Deandra's thumb. Her back feet were propped on Deandra's pinky. The newt was clearly disoriented, though, and her body quickly warmed in Deandra's palm.

"Hey, Sunshine," Deandra said, trying to sound calm despite worrying the newt would melt her hand off.

The sound of Deandra's voice seemed to snap the newt back into lucidity, and her body instantly cooled. She turned her head in a sharp, jerky movement, then cocked it so she could focus one beady black eye on her captor.

Deandra said, "You and I need to have a chat."

# CHAPTER 2

Sunshine hissed at Deandra, but it was clear her heart wasn't in it. She hardly made a sound.

"You've gotta stop harassing people," Deandra said. "After what you've been through, I don't blame you for being angry, but if you keep this up, someone *is* going to call Parks Management on you."

Havoc, who was sitting in front of Deandra and gazing up at the newt in her hand, growled low in his throat.

Deandra turned her wrist so Sunshine faced the dragon. "He knows firsthand how quick someone like Ranger Vicks"—wispy white smoke plumed out of either of Havoc's nostrils—"how someone like Ranger Vicks can pursue criminal charges against sentient and sapient animals." She turned Sunshine back toward herself. "I don't know how *you'd* be classified, but I do know you at least partially understand me. I'm guessing you prefer your freedom to being in a terrarium in Mythic Pet Kitchen or locked up in a Parks Management facility until they decide your fate. If they think you're dangerous, something much worse than being in a cage will happen to you."

Sunshine cocked her head. Deandra could practically see the gears in her amphibian brain churning, but it was anyone's guess what the newt was actually thinking—what she was scheming.

"No more burning holes in clothing, launching out of trees at people, or jumping from bushes to scare people's pets, okay? I'm sure you can figure out how to live a peaceful life in the park without bothering anyone."

Sunshine jerked her head to the side to better scrutinize Deandra with her other eye.

Deandra was rapidly losing faith in her own ability to talk the newt off her chaotic path. "This is all assuming that Chester isn't planning to call Parks Management the moment he gets home."

Sunshine opened her mouth wide, like she was smiling, then started jerking her head back and forth as if listening to a song with a heavy bass beat.

Deandra groaned in dismay. "What the heck are you doing?"

Now Sunshine's head swayed side to side, and she closed her eyes. Before Deandra could ask the newt another rhetorical question, her palm started to heat. Sunshine's body went from cool to warm to scalding with such speed, it was a wonder Deandra managed to quickly deposit the newt on the ground rather than chucking the creature like a football as her instincts had told her to do.

Sunshine's spots went from soft yellow to sunflower to neon. Deandra and Havoc backed away as one.

When Deandra had started her monologue in hopes of getting Sunshine to give up her life of crime, she'd figured it was highly probable that the newt would outright ignore her warnings. The tiny thing taking such offense to Deandra's suggestions that the newt would go *kaboom*—as Chester had feared—hadn't been on her list of possibilities, though.

"Easy, Sunshine," Deandra said, hands up in placation as she took another step back.

Havoc peeped, matching Deandra's backward progression. The fact that Havoc was also nervous about their situation wasn't comforting.

Sunshine seemed to register then that she was freaking them out, and she rolled her eyes. Deandra would have said before that moment that a newt rolling its eyes with all the disdain of a grumpy teenager was impossible, but Axia moved the goalposts on the definition of reality every day.

With a hiss, Sunshine turned toward the bush she'd been occupying earlier. Deandra took that as her cue to leave, but when she took a step away from Sunshine, the newt whipped around and hissed again. Deandra froze.

Sunshine squinted menacingly—which was saying a lot, seeing as she was smaller than Deandra's shoe. When she turned toward the bush, Deandra took a step back, only to have Sunshine scuttle around to face her.

*Hiss!*

"You want me to wait?" Deandra asked.

Sunshine once again rolled her eyes. Her whole body flashed orange for a moment, like the flash of gas-lit flames on a stove. A breath later, she was back to normal, the spots on her back reduced to sunflower yellow rather than neon. Somehow, it came off like a reaction borne out of frustration, like stomping a foot, rather than a threatening one.

"All right, all right," Deandra said, some of the tension leaching from her shoulders. "We'll wait."

With a nod, Sunshine darted into the bush.

The newt, unlike Charles Barksley, made nary a sound while gallivanting in the berry-covered shrubbery. Maybe she was untangling the dog's leash, which would be much appreciated, seeing as Havoc's was now attached to Charles Barksley's harness. Deandra trusted Havoc to stay by her side on the walk home without a leash, but regardless of how well behaved he was, Ranger Vicks would slap her with a ticket should he be out here skulking around, catching her in the act—again—of violating City Ordinance 3-9KM.

When Sunshine emerged from the bush tail-first, she *was* dragging the leash with her. Yet, when she turned around to spit out the leash's clasp, that wasn't the only thing that came out of her mouth. Next to the slightly damp clasp was a coin.

Deandra picked up both items, making sure to hook the leash to Havoc's harness before she examined the coin. It was the size of a quarter in diameter but three times as thick. The coin might have once been shiny gold or copper, but it was coated in grime that she couldn't rub away with her fingertips or scratch off with a nail. It wasn't the greenish patina she was used to seeing on old coins or bronze statues, but rather an unsettling dark reddish film, as if the coin were coated in a layer of dried blood.

The coin didn't bear the face of former presidents, soaring eagles, or historical landmarks. The image in the middle was of a shield with crossed hammers etched in the center. A few runes ringing the outside edge were visible through the grime—at least she thought they were runes. An image adorned the other side as well, but the caked-on film was even thicker than on the front.

If Deandra hadn't been standing in Axia, she would have thought it was a coin that had fallen out of the box of a fantasy-based board game. She could see it being a game piece that represented a cursed piece of pirate booty that needed to be returned to a ghost ship's captain.

She stilled.

*Oh gosh. What if this really* was *cursed pirate gold?*

She flinched when Sunshine was suddenly standing on her forearm. Had she leaped up there, or had she scaled the length of Deandra's body so lightly and quickly that Deandra hadn't noticed?

The coin was propped between Deandra's pointer finger and thumb. Sunshine scuttled forward so she could pat the coin's face with her sticky digits. She cocked her head so she could watch Deandra closely with one beady eye.

"Is this for me?"

*Hiss.*

"Thank you?"

Sunshine rolled her eye, seemingly once again put out by Deandra's slow wit. The newt tapped the coin with a foot again, tapped her own face once, hissed, then, without warning, launched off Deandra's hand and into the bush like a high diver into a pool.

Deandra didn't move for a full minute, just in case the newt was in there fetching more treasure. When she didn't skitter back out, Deandra tentatively gave Havoc's leash a tug. They took a few cautious steps away from the bushes, but Sunshine didn't come charging back out.

Hoping the newt would take Deandra's warnings to heart, Deandra and Havoc set off for home, Deandra turning the strange coin over and over between her fingers.

DEANDRA WOULD HAVE DEPOSITED the strange coin in a drawer and never thought of it again had it not started humming faintly in her car's cup holder on the way home. Havoc heard the strange sound, too, and stood on the back seat, head between the front seats, growling low.

"Any guesses, boy?"

Havoc chirped once in reply, which told Deandra exactly nothing.

The coin was still humming faintly when Deandra pulled into a parking spot at Wendy's apartment complex.

Leaving the coin where it lay, Deandra quickly climbed out of the car and then extracted Havoc from the back seat. The pair stood beside the open driver's-side door, staring in.

"What if it's like a tiny magical bomb?" Deandra asked Havoc. "Sunshine likes fire and making things explode, doesn't she?"

But Deandra remembered all over again that, even if Sunshine *was* unhinged, a lot of her admittedly terrible behavior had been the result of her former owner placing Sunshine under an invasive, forced familiar bond, essentially turning the newt into an amphibious assassin. It was also true that the newt had a predisposition for mayhem; the repeated harassment of Chester and Charles Barksley was done of her own volition.

But given the overbearing personality of man and canine alike, Deandra couldn't *entirely* blame Sunshine for taking her frustrations out on the pair.

So if Deandra gave Sunshine the benefit of the doubt, the humming coin wasn't going to blow her hand off if she picked it up again. She recalled the fate that had befallen Wendy's car a mere two weeks ago when Sunshine had set the thing ablaze with Wendy and Deandra still in it. Insurance companies in hubs worked remarkably fast, though, and Wendy had been in a new car in under a week following the incident. Deandra, however, hadn't switched to a hub insurance company yet and would need to deal with mundane companies should her own car go up in flames.

That, even more than the fear of losing a limb, was what

compelled her to reach back into her car. Resting a knee on the seat long enough to stick her hand into the cup holder, she grabbed the coin and then hurried back out.

Instead of sunlight glinting off the surface of the coin, the dingy face somehow appeared even darker than it had earlier. Deandra turned it over and over between her fingers, hoping the constant handling would loosen the muck covering it. She wasn't sure if it was a good sign or not that the coin stopped humming once it was in Deandra's hand. Was this like a bomb's countdown clock hitting zero, and now she existed in a moment of suspended animation before it exploded and leveled the parking lot?

Her less morbid thought, though no less bizarre, was that somehow the coin was comforted by being held, and its earlier humming had been due to distress.

Sentient currency? Deandra wasn't sure her nerves were ready for that.

Havoc had stopped growling when the coin's humming stopped, and now he sat by her feet, staring up at her with his head canted.

Deandra lowered the coin so it was nostril-level with Havoc, allowing him to give it a good sniff. After a few cautious inhales, Havoc shook his head sharply and snorted out a plume of white smoke in distaste. The reaction wasn't as violent as the one he'd had when encountering purple cabbage for the first time, but it was close.

She pulled the coin away.

With a shrug, she closed her car door and headed for the apartment. Wendy wouldn't be home for another couple of hours, but maybe she'd have an idea about the odd coin.

Once inside and settled, she considered leaving the coin on the dining room table for Wendy to inspect later. But Deandra's worries about potential magical explosions made her keep the item in hand.

Wendy was a very patient and understanding person, but

Deandra wouldn't blame her for being cross if Deandra brought home a gift from a dodgy, mildly homicidal fire newt that then took out a city block, including her home and everything in it.

Deandra wondered, not for the first time, if her life in Axia would ever be normal.

# CHAPTER 3

Deandra only allowed Wendy a few minutes to get situated after she got home from work before ambushing her. Though the coin had been perfectly still and quiet for the past two hours, Deandra's nerves were shot, and there was a faint imprint of the coin's diameter etched into her palm because she hadn't let it go.

"Hi!" Deandra said, rushing up behind her cousin, who had

just pulled out the fixings for an emergency sandwich since she'd forgotten to pack lunch that day.

Wendy flinched hard and knocked a tomato off the counter. It landed with a muted thud. Havoc was upon it in seconds, tomato juice dripping off his chin.

Whirling with a knife in one hand and her other slapped over her heart, Wendy said, "What the heck is wrong with you? Don't sneak up on people when they're armed! I could have stabbed you to death."

Deandra eyed the butter knife her cousin clutched and the smear of mayonnaise on the dull blade. Given the way Havoc was snuffling loudly by their feet, he was probably licking up a larger glob that had hit the floor.

"Sorry! But something weird happened at the park, and I've been stressed out ever since, and I need your expertise in magical stuff because what if I've been holding a bomb for two hours?" Deandra asked in a rush.

Wendy stared blankly at her. "I've lived here for nearly a year, and these sorts of things have never happened to me."

"On my first day here, you yelled at Allegra at the Welcome Center because you knew she'd given me a 'crash course' on Axia. A lady turning into a swan the size of an ostrich is weird as all get-out, Wendy, but you're so used to it now, you think it's normal."

Wendy considered that. "Huh. I guess you're right." Giving her head a little shake, she said, "Okay, wait. Did you say magical *bomb*?"

"See!" Deandra said. "*That* should have been the first thing you commented on." She held out her right hand in Wendy's direction, palm up, revealing the coin.

"Ooh, interesting." A few moments later, Wendy cautiously met Deandra's eye, giving her a look that suggested she thought Deandra might have suffered a concussion. "I know it's kind of crusty, but that's a coin, Dee."

"Well, I know *that*." Moving to a stretch of countertop not occupied by produce and condiment bottles, Deandra carefully laid the coin down and then took several steps back.

"What are you—*oh*. Is it ... humming?"

Havoc padded toward the coin's location. He kept all four feet on the floor, but he glared up at the lip of the countertop and growled softly.

Deandra asked, "So you don't recognize the shield design? Humming currency isn't a normal thing here?"

Wendy took up a spot beside Havoc, hands on her knees so she could get a closer look at the coin. "Not that I know of. Where did you find it?"

They both kept a wary eye on the coin—which Wendy was sure *wasn't* a bomb—as they made sandwiches. Deandra told her about the altercation at the park and how the fire newt had seemingly given the coin to Deandra as a gift.

Before taking her plate to the dining room table, Deandra snatched up the humming disc. When she touched it, the humming stopped. When she placed it on the table beside her lunch, the humming immediately resumed.

Havoc took up his usual place below the table with his head on Deandra's foot. The vibration of his low, continuous growl tickled her toes.

Wendy said, "My best guess is that it's a talisman of some kind, not currency. Usually, when you want to lock a spell into an object, the item has to be small. The magic is more stable when it's confined; it can get erratic and try to break free if the space it's in is too big. That's why talismans are usually trinket-shaped—jewelry, keys, stones ..."

"Coins," Deandra said, shooting another glance at the object in question.

"Coins," Wendy agreed. "But one that reacts to *not* being handled is the opposite of how talismans usually work. Not being in use typically makes them go dormant, while contact wakes up the magic."

Deandra thought of the travel talisman Wendy had sent her weeks ago. When it was in the box it had been shipped in, the swirling magic in the hollow of the disc-shaped pendant had been calm. When Deandra had touched it, though, the magic roared to quiet life, like a contained windstorm.

"I don't know if this is actually from fae realm lore or if I read it in a novel," Wendy said slowly, brain clearly in overdrive, "but I remember something about dwarven coins that were alive. Not that they could talk or feel, but that the metal they were forged from came from a mine where the gold ore had been shot through with veins of liquid magic."

Deandra both did *and* didn't want that to be true. She couldn't shake the feeling that the coin was upset somehow, which was honestly ridiculous. She hated the idea that there was a kind of consciousness in the disc, that it was humming out of loneliness.

Wendy scarfed down the rest of her sandwich, then hastily wiped her mouth and fingers on a napkin. She was either jazzed by this new mystery, or the sandwich had given her a shot of post-work energy. "Even though I just left, the best person I know of to ask what this thing is would be my boss, Heather. The shop is open for another three hours or so. Heather's a walking encyclopedia of talismans. Even if she can't tell us exactly what it is, she could tell us what it *isn't*, which could be just as helpful."

Deandra stared at her cousin. "Is this really how you want to spend your evening?"

Wendy shrugged. "Why not? Plus, I know you. You're worried about something happening to Sunshine, even if she *is* a tiny demon who tried to murder us. You don't want her to get snatched up by Parks Management—especially not by Ranger Vicks."

Havoc's constant low growl went up in intensity for a moment at the sound of the park ranger's name.

Wendy continued, "Sunshine can't keep harassing people in the park if she doesn't want to end up behind bars." Her eyes grew huge. "Oh my gosh. Can you imagine a jail cell the size of a terrarium?"

"Focus," Deandra chided, though she, too, was amused by the image of a tiny cell. Her faint smile faded as she pictured Sunshine with her little feet wrapped around bars, the spots on her back dulled to a sickly yellow.

"Maybe Sunshine really *was* just giving you a present," Wendy said. "But she doesn't seem like a gift-giving kind of newt. For all we know, she hasn't been purposely harassing people. Maybe she's trying to give them a message, but she's going about it like only a psychopathic, fire-wielding amphibian can."

Deandra considered that. Recalling the almost gleeful look in Sunshine's eye as she rode Charles Barksley's head like a hat, the small dog shrieking in terror, Deandra figured the newt had been fueled by a love of chaos more than attempting to pass on helpful information.

All the same, the newt *had* seemed exasperated with Deandra for not understanding the significance of the coin. Even if she hadn't been trying to give Chester anything but heart palpitations, Deandra believed there was a message the newt was trying to impart to *her*.

"You really do need to lay off the true crime stuff," Deandra said. "You get too excited by the prospect of solving a mystery."

Wendy scoffed. "As if your eyes didn't light up when I suggested we go talk to Heather."

It was annoying how well her cousin knew her.

"Yeah, yeah," Deandra said. "We going or not?"

Wendy grinned.

HEATHER'S ELIXIRS catered to witches in need of supplies for their potions and spells but also to mundanes who could purchase low-level magical tinctures and talismans that allowed them to experience a bit of magic themselves. The first time Deandra had been in the shop, she'd been distracted, what with Grimshaw Peabody screaming his head off at Heather. She'd noted then, though, as she did now, that the shop didn't smell heavily of incense or patchouli or lavender, as mundane new-agey shops often did.

Heather's Elixirs smelled faintly of sugar and vanilla for some reason, reminding Deandra of a cupcake shop. The layout wasn't as cluttered as many mundane shops of its kind either. It felt more like a mom-and-pop general store. Even so, Deandra figured it had been a good call to leave Havoc at home for this outing. Per the sign by the front door, pets were welcome in the shop, but Deandra didn't want to risk scaring the clientele with Havoc's dire wolf form, nor did she trust his tail not to knock everything off the low shelves.

Madison was behind the counter. She managed to glance up from her phone when Deandra and Wendy walked in, but upon seeing who had entered the shop, remained expressionless. Then her attention went back to her phone. Deandra wondered what the young lady's job prospects would be if she weren't Heather's niece.

Shaking her head, Deandra cast her gaze around the shop. Two walls were lined with built-in cubbyholes, the wood painted a fresh white. The cubbies on one wall were filled with various dried flowers and herbs. Each cubby had a label stating not only the type of plant, but its medicinal or magical properties as well as its most common uses. Deandra wondered why the smell wafting from that wall alone wasn't cloying. She assumed magic was at play somehow.

The wall opposite was lined with talismans arranged by type. Since travel talismans were the only type Deandra was familiar with, she expected those to be the most common, but unlocking talismans took up the most space. An unlocking talisman could be spelled to recognize a specific lock—replacing a person's house key, for example—but couldn't be used as a universal skeleton key that opened multiple locks. Deandra imagined ten different necklace talismans hanging around her neck, like a marathoner proudly displaying their many medals, and decided she'd just stick to her ring of mundane keys.

Several freestanding tables and counters ran along the middle of the shop. Here, there were books about various talismans, how-to guides on making your own talisman, and books on potioncraft for a wide range of skill levels. A bright red sign near a stack of advanced potioncraft books stated that they could only be purchased if the customer provided proof that they'd completed an intermediate course offered by an accredited academy of magical learning or from a local witch who went by "Scott the Magus."

Potion-making supplies were available in abundance. Sizes of glass vials ranged from no bigger than an adult's thumb to nearly three feet tall. There were baskets of cork stoppers and plastic caps and sheets of frinsel wax that, when exposed to high heat, freezing temperatures, or bubbling acid, could be used to seal the mouth of a bottle. Deandra hoped that meant that frinsel wax also kept the bubbling acid *in* the bottle.

She was sure that if she ever attended one of the potion-making classes held in the shop, she would melt her face from her skull.

Wendy only allowed Deandra a few minutes of perusing the store in quiet fascination before she pulled her away from a display of metals and toward Heather's office. The metals were so pretty, though! They came in cubes, and in short, fat cylinders, and in bars. She recognized copper, iron, and steel, but there were metals that shimmered blue and purple and green. There was a bowl of pink-colored ball bearings that looked for all the world like a bowl of sugary kid's cereal, only the bearings seemed to be vibrating, occasionally giving the illusion that the metal had liquefied.

Despite being near the odd-acting metal in the bowl, the coin in Deandra's pocket remained dormant—like a content cat curled up in a sunbeam.

What if Sunshine gave Deandra the coin because she'd grown weary of how needy it was? If Deandra was forced to adopt a sentient coin on top of a precocious baby dragon, would she need to keep the item on her at all times? Would boring a hole into the coin so Deandra could fashion it into a necklace *hurt* the coin somehow?

"Come in!" called Heather from the other side of the office door, snapping Deandra out of her thoughts.

Wendy let herself in.

Heather was seated behind her desk, reading glasses perched low on her nose as she squinted at her laptop's screen. The squinting suggested she needed a better prescription.

Heather glanced up as the cousins entered her office and cocked her head, clearly confused. Pushing her jade-rimmed glasses into her hair, she closed her laptop with a soft snick and folded her arms on top of it. Her dark hair that had gone nearly entirely gray spilled around her shoulders. "Did you forget something, Wendy?" Her gaze flicked over to Deandra. "Is everything okay?"

Once the cousins were inside and Wendy had closed the door again, Wendy excitedly recounted Deandra's encounter in the park.

By the end of the tale, Heather's eyes were wide, and she was on her feet. "Can I see it?"

Deandra pulled the coin from her pocket and placed it in front of Heather, right over the logo on her laptop's lid. The second Deandra's fingers left the metal, the humming started up.

The sound didn't last long, however, as Heather snatched up the coin almost immediately to examine it. The coin's protests quieted.

"How interesting!" Heather said, her tone reverent.

She said nothing else for two full minutes, using a mundane-looking magnifying glass and then a jeweler's loupe to study the muck-encrusted images on both sides of the coin, the runes, and even the faint ridges that etched the coin's edge. Deandra did her best not to fidget as she waited, debating about pulling out her phone to play Lollipop Jumble. It would have made the time pass much faster than merely staring at the ticking second hand of the clock on the wall behind Heather's desk. Wendy gently gnawed on a cuticle.

When Heather finally glanced up from the coin, the sudden movement startled the cousins out of their stupors.

"Would you be okay with me soaking the coin in a solvent, Deandra?" Heather asked.

Deandra's brain glitched. The coin wasn't *truly* hers, even if the newt had given it to her. For all Deandra knew, Sunshine was a thief and had stolen it out of some unsuspecting person's pocket, then pawned the hot item off on Deandra, who was now an accessory to a crime. What if this truly was a rare bit of priceless fae pirate currency, like a piece of eight—but magical—and whatever concoction Heather dropped the coin into dissolved part of history?

"Dee?" Wendy asked from beside her. "Come back to Earth ..."

Before Deandra could answer, Heather said, "I should have clarified that the solvent would only work to remove the grime coating the coin, not damage the metal itself. This is dwarven aureate, if I'm not mistaken. It's from the fae realm. The story goes that there was an alchemist who was so radical in his ideas that he was shunned by society everywhere he went. He used living subjects for his alchemical experiments, which resulted in the death of a great number of people—for lack of a better term—*and* animals.

"He eventually set up his final alchemy lab in a mountain range in a remote area of a dwarven territory. One day, one of his dangerous experiments went too far, and an explosion leveled his entire facility and everything in it—including himself. The runoff of magical and chemical byproducts from the explosion supposedly made its way into the river at the base of the mountain range, slowly changing the flora and fauna of the region over time. One of those changes was the chemical runoff seeping into rocks already rich with gold.

"Years later, a group of dwarven environmentalists were in the region to study the effects of the explosion—a study that hadn't been conducted in some time due to the remoteness of the area. Not to mention the magically mutated animals that now roamed the area and had been doing so for at least a century without the intervention of people.

"It was during that expedition that gold was found in one of the riverbeds—gold that had strange magical properties. The metal, though not sentient, per se, seemed to have a life of its own. It seemed to alter its properties depending on the person who interacted with it. Gold, being malleable and heavy, is a terrible choice for weapon craft.

"Yet one of the dwarven kings, upon discovery of the magical gold, tasked his personal blacksmith with making a sword out of it. The blacksmith succeeded—the only one to ever do so, from what I've read. I believe she went into hiding after that ... unless, of course, she vanished from history because the king wanted to ensure no one else ever had a weapon as formidable as his. The dwarven king was rumored to have slaughtered his way across the dwarven lands, snatching up territory left and right with that unbreakable magical golden sword held in his fist. The depictions of the Golden Dwarven King must have been a sight to behold."

Wendy let out a low whistle. "I'm very proud of myself for not being totally wrong about magic dwarven gold. Good job, memory!"

Deandra's mind, however, was focused on the blacksmith in the king's employ who had crafted the golden weapon. Had she been haunted by what she'd made? Had she thought the king merely wanted a decorative sword to hang on the wall as a sign of his wealth, but instead she'd given him a tool that aided in altering dwarven history forever? Had the king threatened her—or her family—if she didn't do as he bade?

Deandra hoped she'd escaped and that the king hadn't snuffed out her life to further cement his own legacy.

"Would it be okay to soak it in solvent, Deandra?" Heather asked again, forcing Deandra to let go of the image in her mind of a disillusioned blacksmith running through dark deserted streets, tears streaming down her face. "I'm sure the designs on both sides are just lovely."

Deandra noted that Heather had never once stated she thought there was anything magical about the disc, other than the gold it was forged from. "Do you think it's only a coin, then? Not a talisman?"

Heather's lips thinned minutely at the use of "only" as an adjective for the dwarven coin. "I'm honestly not sure if either label is accurate, but I'll know more once it's clean."

Deandra nodded tightly, still worried that this so-called solvent would melt the coin to goo. What if the coin screamed in agony the whole time?

And yet, just like when she'd heard thumping from inside a dumpster in the back of a deserted parking lot, she inched toward the unknown rather than away from it.

Curiosity was a dangerous thing.

Steeling herself, she asked, "How long will the solvent take?"

Heather, beaming and with coin in hand, skirted her desk and headed for the office door without answering the question. The excited gleam in the otherwise reserved woman's eye gave Deandra pause.

With a flourish, Heather pulled open the door. "Follow me, ladies!"

Wendy and Deandra, standing shoulder to shoulder, stared after Heather, who was hotfooting it across the shop.

"I'm not sure if I've ever seen her move that fast," Wendy said, bewildered. "Should we be worried? I mean, unique magical trinkets are the main things in this world that get her juices going, but maybe this is too *much* juice."

"Please stop saying 'juice,'" Deandra said.

Wendy barreled on, undeterred. "Is this like taking a person who's on a diet to a cupcake shop and setting them loose?"

"Bringing it to Heather was *your* idea," Deandra said. "If this goes sideways, it's entirely your fault."

Wendy scoffed in mock offense. "It's *your* fault for befriending an unhinged newt."

She supposed her cousin had a point. As a general life rule, it was probably unwise to accept gifts from shifty newts.

"I'd better get the classroom ready," Wendy said. "We got a new shipment of extra-large sheets of frinsel wax mats to put on the floor during potion-making classes. We're hoping it'll minimize how many holes get burned into the wood. Won't solve the problem of how often the ceiling gets scorched, though. Scrubbing off magical soot is *not* a fun job, by the way. Especially since I missed a spot last week and now there are bright blue mushrooms growing in the corner. They're impervious to fire."

Deandra turned to stare at the side of her cousin's head. "That right there is what I'm talking about. Magical soot? Fire-resistant blue mushrooms? That's weird, Wendy! You're unfazed by weird."

Heather was hauling tail back in their direction now, several glass bottles clanking around in the basket she'd procured from near the front door. Stopping a few feet from the doorway, she looked in at Deandra and Wendy, incredulous that they'd yet to move. "I need a bucket of hyssin acid, Wendy. And do be careful. Madison was careless yesterday and grabbed the hyssin acid instead of yengrass oil—the bottles are clearly labeled!—and melted my favorite ceramic bowl. It's still fused to a table."

Without another word, Heather bustled toward the left into a section of the store Deandra had yet to see.

Wendy jumped to attention and hurried out of the office and toward the right, presumably in the direction of the storage room. Reluctantly, Deandra followed her, hoping she hadn't doomed the coin to a fate even worse than that of the melted ceramic bowl.

# CHAPTER 4

The storage room was as big as Deandra's bedroom in Wendy's apartment. Three walls were lined with shelves stuffed to the gills with supplies. The fourth wall had a massive worktable pressed up against it and was covered in what Deandra assumed were talisman-making odds and ends. The room was cluttered in a way that made Deandra twitchy. It looked like a mad scientist's lab from a cartoon—colorful and chaotic. Magic didn't zing in the air like electricity—though even if it did, Deandra knew her mundane senses wouldn't be able to pick up on it—but there was something otherworldly about the feel of the space all the same.

Deandra was happy to loiter in the doorway until Wendy located the bucket of hyssin acid. The bucket in question was made of opaque white plastic, along with a lid made of the same material, and it was outfitted with a handle. The label was merely a stretch of masking tape with the word **HYSSIN** written in all caps in thick black ink.

The handle looked rather flimsy to Deandra's untrained eye, so she gave Wendy a wide berth as she led the way past Heather's office and presumably toward the classroom, the bucket hanging near her knee. A door stood ajar straight ahead, but Wendy strolled past it and took a right into the hallway. Beyond the door, the sound of popcorn popping in the microwave sounded like distant gunfire. They passed the employee bathrooms next and then came to a stop at a closed and unmarked door.

Given the size of Heather's Elixirs from the outside, Deandra couldn't imagine the classroom was very large.

When Wendy opened the door, however, Deandra froze in the doorway, slack-jawed.

Deandra had often wondered how such a magic-filled town, packed with beings plucked from a fantasy world, stayed contained in a place as relatively small as Axia. And then she'd see places like this—places that didn't make sense as far as mundane physics went. Were there talismans embedded in the walls, floor, and ceiling to give the space more square footage than should have been possible? Deandra figured if such talismans existed, someone like Heather—a supposed expert in the magical trinkets—would either know where to find them or how to make them herself.

The classroom was as large as the main shop itself, which made absolutely no sense to Deandra. By stepping into the room, was she stepping into an area that existed in a different plane some-how? Was walking into this magicked place similar to teleporting?

If she walked to the right-hand side of the room that presumably shared a wall with the main shop, would Madison at her post behind the register hear Deandra if she knocked on the plaster?

Wendy had only made it halfway into the classroom when she turned around, having realized Deandra was loitering in yet another doorway. "Oh gosh. Sorry, Dee. I forgot you hadn't been in here before." She doubled back. "Is your brain about to explode?"

Deandra shook herself out of her wonder, if only because Wendy's proximity meant the bucket of hyssin acid was nearby again. She shot a glance at Wendy's hand casually holding the handle of the opaque bucket. She pulled her gaze away to settle on Wendy's face. "How?" was all she could get out.

"No idea. I mean, I know it's a combo of talismans scattered all over the place and runes etched into the walls and floor," Wendy said. "I think this space was no bigger than a broom closet before magic expanded it. Don't ask me if we're in a pocket dimension because I don't know. I may seem like I'm super cool with all this magic stuff, but I also learned a while ago that sometimes it's better not to ask questions, so you don't have an existential crisis."

Deandra swallowed hard and bobbed her head. "Got it. I'm good not knowing details about this one."

"Smart," Wendy said, then turned on her heel and headed farther into the room.

Wiping her clammy hands down the thighs of her jeans, Deandra gave herself a full-body fortifying shake, then followed her cousin. She only flinched a *little* when the door she'd been holding open snicked closed behind her.

The majority of the space was taken up by three massive wooden tables, the legs as wide as telephone poles. Deandra wondered if the tables needed to be extra sturdy to withstand the magical nonsense that went on in here on what seemed to be a regular basis. On the back of the nearest table, she spotted the ceramic bowl that didn't look fused to the table so much as rather straight-up liquefied.

She glanced up then, curious if she could find the supposed patch of glowing blue mushrooms. What she noticed first were the large chandeliers that looked like something Heather might have picked up at a medieval-chic home-goods store. One hung above each table from thick steel chains, and each was encased in a cage-like metal covering.

She stopped in her tracks as she realized the ceiling was even taller here than in the main shop. Beyond being unnerved that Wendy had to climb ladders that tall to scrub wooden slats free of magical soot, the mere fact that the ceilings in this room and the main shop weren't level, yet the difference wasn't noticeable from the building's exterior, was making Deandra's head hurt again.

She diverted her gaze toward her feet as she walked, but she soon regretted that choice, too. She quickly spotted random patches of wooden flooring that didn't match the area around it. These were likely the spots that had been burned away by some magical mishap or other.

The floor wasn't doing a *full* impression of a patchwork quilt, but it was getting close. Could hyssin acid do that?

Deandra yanked her gaze up and kept it locked on Wendy. Wendy was a safe thing to look at—other than the bucket of highly corrosive acid in her hand, anyway.

Heather had set up her mini mad scientist lab on the middle table. The bookend tables' surfaces were bare other than a handful of lit candles—well, and the melted bowl. The medieval fixtures above provided plenty of light, even if it was mildly creepy, so Deandra figured the candles were more for ambiance than anything else.

"Come, come, ladies," Heather said, glancing up from her workstation long enough to wave them over.

Most of the seating was backless stools that were shoved under the table. Wendy and Deandra stood across from Heather. Wendy reached across the table to carefully place the hyssin acid near the large light-green place mat Heather had arranged her tools on. Deandra wondered if the place mat was actually a sheet of frinsel wax. It *would* be a shame if the acid burned a hole through the gorgeous table.

On the sheet were brushes—some soft and some wire—Q-tips, pliers, tweezers, three types of magnifying glasses, and several small metal bowls full of liquids of different colors. Heather carefully pulled the top off the hyssin acid and dipped a glittering steel-colored ladle into it. It was then that Deandra registered that Heather wore gloves. They looked thick—like something one would wear in the snow—but they didn't seem to impede dexterity.

The acid was a sickly yellow, and it popped and spat as the ladle was placed inside. Heather carefully spooned a healthy portion into a bowl, then snapped the acid's lid back in place. She deposited the ladle in an empty bowl.

The area in the middle of the place mat was left empty, Deandra presumed, for the coin.

Heather smiled at Deandra. She looked like a kid on Christmas morning. "You ready for this?"

"Go for it," Deandra said, plastering on a tight smile, still worried about the coin's well-being as if it really were alive.

Beaming, Heather extracted the coin from her pocket and placed it in the middle of the mat. The humming began immediately. Hooking a stool out from under the table with a foot with practiced ease, Heather smiled down at the coin. "Don't you worry. We'll get you cleaned up in no time."

Wendy and Deandra glanced at each other and shrugged, then pulled out stools as well.

"No time" ended up being close to an hour.

Wendy got roped into helping in the shop several times by a bewildered Madison who kept peeking into the classroom to ask for help. By the third time Wendy's assistance was requested,

Deandra hoped she wouldn't need to bail her cousin out of jail later.

Mostly because Deandra's bank account was in no state for such things.

Deandra kept herself occupied by playing Lollipop Jumble and occasionally handing Heather items when she asked for them—like a surgeon's assistant. Deandra's anxiety about what this deep cleaning was doing to the coin's soul or whatever had gone away almost entirely as soon as Heather started the process, as the coin either stayed silent or gently purred like a cat.

Yes, *purred*.

Axia was an endless fountain of weird.

Wendy was back and seated beside Deandra when Heather finally declared, "All done!"

The cousins glanced up sharply from their respective phones. Wendy had finally caved and downloaded the game, too. She'd whispered, "Why would you introduce me to this addicting nightmare, Deandra Hendricks?!" under her breath after the first few levels.

Heather, with the coin lying flat on her palm, stood so she could lean across the table.

Deandra hastily deposited her phone on the table and stood as well, reaching for the coin. She gently took it from Heather, who looked a bit bereft about giving it up. The metal, surprisingly, was a metallic blue. She wondered if that was due to the alchemical runoff that had infused itself into the rocks.

It was so beautiful, it almost seemed like in insult to the metal that it had been crafted into a mere coin.

Wendy was on her feet as well, her arm pressed to Deandra's as she leaned in to get a better look.

The image of a shield with crossed hammers etched in the center was so detailed, Deandra swore she could make out the wood grain on the shield's body and see sunlight winking off a few of the rivets that were welded into its metal frame. She had been right; runes *did* run along the outside edge of the coin. They were written in two nested circles.

"Any idea what the runes mean?" Deandra asked, glancing up at Heather.

"I'm honestly not sure they *are* runes. Not the way we understand them here in the earthen realm, anyway," Heather said. "I'd need to study it some more to be sure, but my gut tells me those symbols are Dwarvish."

Deandra blinked dumbly at her. She was still slowly working through the welcome booklet Allegra had given her on her first day in Axia, which included a brief history of not only the town, but the hub system at large. "What, like this was made by a dwarf from the fae realm, and it ended up here because it was, I don't know, in a dwarf's pocket when the Glitch happened, and the dwarf ended up marooned here?"

Heather nodded, thoughtful. "That would be my guess."

Even if the coin couldn't be used in this realm as currency, Deandra had to assume that it would hold priceless sentimental value for dwarves here. It was the kind of piece that belonged in a museum of dwarven history, not in the bushes at Oracle Park being guarded by a loopy fire newt.

Returning her focus to the coin, Deandra flipped it over, still unsure if an image actually graced the other side, as it had previously been too covered in grime to tell.

There *was* an image on the back.

Wendy sucked in a gasp. Deandra's knees went a little wobbly.

"What is it?" Heather asked, concerned.

There, on the back of the coin, was an etching of a ball of flame. The design wasn't nearly as impressive, detail-wise, as the shield on the other side. But it was the relative simplicity that had allowed Deandra—and Wendy—to recognize it in an instant.

The ball of flame was identical to the one etched on the tag that hung from Havoc's collar.

# CHAPTER 5

"All right, one of you ladies needs to tell me what all the fuss is about," Heather said, after Deandra and Wendy merely stared at the coin for several long seconds. "Do you recognize the symbol?"

Deandra didn't have the first clue what to tell Heather. She wasn't the best liar on the planet to begin with, but when under pressure, she had a tendency to blurt out the truth at inopportune times. She literally bit down on her tongue to keep Havoc's secrets tucked away in her mouth.

Luckily for her, Wendy was far better at thinking quickly under pressure—unless they were confronting murderers or arsonists, anyway. And really, who could blame a girl for panicking then?

Wendy playfully nudged Deandra's arm and laughed. "You thought it was the emblem for the fire elemental clan on *Gavin's Hollow*, too, didn't you?"

What on earth was *Gavin's Hollow*? Wendy nudged her a little harder. "*Oh!*" Deandra yelped. "Oh, yes. That *totally* looks like their clan calling card."

Deandra mentally winced at how stilted she sounded.

Wendy nodded sagely, then smiled at Heather. "New show we're obsessed with."

Any curiosity Heather seemed to harbor went out of her like the tide. "Goddess above, Wendy, I don't know how you can be obsessed with *this* many shows." She waved a dismissive hand. "I don't have time for TV."

Wendy nodded again, as if she'd expected that reply.

"Is it okay if I make a few rubbings of the coin, Deandra?" Heather asked. "I can do some research on the symbols in my off hours."

Deandra resisted the urge to point out that "off hours" was the perfect time to watch TV. She handed the coin back to Heather, briefly worried the woman was going to snatch it, cackle like a witch from a cartoon, and skedaddle.

Coin in hand, Heather gave herself a few more seconds to admire it. "Let's head back to my office. I'll clean up this mess later," she said, wrinkling her nose at the frinsel wax mat dotted with dirty paper towels, cotton balls, and Q-tips; scattered clumps of whatever gunk had once coated the coin; and a sea of bowls, brushes, and tweezers. Even though most of the cleaning implements looked mundane, they must have been magical in nature, as the hyssin acid hadn't reduced them all to ash.

Heather was off again, long strides taking her across the classroom.

The cousins didn't move until the sound of Heather's footfalls were cut off by the door closing behind her.

Deandra whirled toward Wendy, who turned toward her at the same time.

"That's the same symbol on Havoc's tag, right?" they asked in unison.

Deandra gusted out a breath. "What does it mean? Does it mean *anything*? What if it's like, I don't know, a business logo or something? Maybe the ball of flame is the Starbucks of metallic products. Both the coin and his collar tag are made out of metal ..."

Wendy shot Deandra a dubious glance. "You think some dwarven family in the fae realm has such a monopoly on metal manufacturing that they make coins *and* dog tags? Plus, it seems like the collar is relatively new, right? And that coin is either super old, or it wasn't treated very well. And! If it *did* come from the fae realm, and the Glitch happened at least a century ago, why would a second-, third-, fourth-generation dwarf still be using that symbol? The shield on the other side looks like a family crest, so I can see using that because of family pride or whatever, but the ball of flame symbol is almost generic."

Deandra mulled that over. "So what are you saying, exactly?"

Wendy shrugged. "Oh, I have no idea whatsoever."

Deandra huffed out a laugh.

They hurried out of the classroom to find Heather.

"Finally," Heather said without looking up as Deandra and Wendy stepped into her office.

She was seated behind her desk, her laptop open again, glasses perched on the end of her nose. They weren't mundane reading glasses this time, though; the right lens had a steampunk-esque attachment over the glass. When she glanced up, Deandra flinched at Heather's huge owl-like right eye, blown up to three times its usual diameter.

Heather shoved the glasses into her hair. "So! I actually had a hunch about the ball of flame symbol and hoped you two came to the same conclusion. You were acting so strangely, I thought you were on the same track. But alas, your hunch led you to *Gabriel's Haven.*" She tsked in disappointment. "Anyway, the symbol looked an awful lot like the signature of blacksmith Ingrid Varros, so I was doing a little research on her while you two were dillydallying for ages."

Deandra resisted the urge to say that they hadn't left her alone for longer than ten minutes. This fired-up woman was not the same meek lady Deandra had met only weeks ago when she was being berated by grumpy Grimshaw Peabody. Deandra supposed most people came alive when they were in their element, though, and Heather was clearly passionate about obscure fae history and magical items.

"Was Ingrid a master blacksmith?" Wendy asked, clearly choosing to ignore Heather's uncharacteristic sassiness.

"She *is* a master blacksmith," Heather said. "She was born in this realm. Her great-grandfather wound up here during the Glitch and thankfully passed his knowledge down to his children and grandchildren. Ingrid has made quite the name for herself. The ball of flame symbol became her signature of sorts, and she's added it to many of her creations—weaponry, talismans, armor. Her great-grandfather got her started, but if I remember correctly, she was also an apprentice to Phillip *Grantham*, of all people." Heather whistled appreciatively to herself.

She must have seen Deandra's blank expression mirrored on Wendy's face because she huffed.

"You're honestly telling me, Wendy, that you watch all these television shows and have never heard of Phillip Grantham? He's a world-renowned armorer! He's won fourteen Tillys *and* a Sheba for the armor he created for the actors in all eight seasons of *Bengal's Army*."

"You mean *Rengal's Army*?" Wendy asked. "Because if so, holy crap, that show is incredible."

Deandra, once again, was lost. Even though she still had well over a dozen seasons of *Faet of the Heart* to watch, her list of what to binge next had tripled during this visit alone—though she wasn't sure if *Gavin's Hollow* was a real show or one plucked from Wendy's fertile imagination.

Heather offered an exasperated sigh before her focus shifted to her laptop. She clacked away at the keyboard for a few seconds. "According to this," she said slowly as her typing stopped, her eyes scanning the screen, "Ingrid started creating expensive pieces for shows, movies, and private collectors about ten years ago—that's when she started using the ball of flame signature. I don't know if the fame and prestige went to her head, but she started acting a bit strangely during the last few years. Perhaps that's par for the course for young celebrities who suddenly come into a lot of money.

"Anyway, one of her most notable quirks was that she began amassing a menagerie of rare fire-aligned animals. She claimed the fire produced by living fae and magic-touched animals held properties that went beyond traditional means. She believed that, with the combination of their fire, her collection of unique fae metals, and her own exceptional skill set, she could craft items never before seen in the fae realm *or* this one."

Deandra's mind kept frantically circling back to "menagerie of rare fire-aligned animals." If "dragon" didn't fit that description, Deandra didn't know what did.

Had *Ingrid* been Havoc's previous owner?

"There was a lot of speculation that Ingrid had blasted past eccentric and perhaps suffered a mental break," Heather said.

"When she up and vanished from the spotlight a year or so ago, a lot of people feared the worst. But it also played into the theory that her fame and fortune had ruined her. There *still* hasn't been much news about her. She abandoned several projects with big clients. Grantham was paid *a lot* of money to be her fill-in on a movie coming out next year. She bailed on scheduled TV appearances and interviews with no notice, things like that.

"According to this article, while there *have* been a few sightings of her, they span nearly a dozen hubs. Telepad travel makes the sheer distance between sightings plausible, but I don't know how many have been substantiated. There are a few pictures, but none of them are that clear. The average hub citizen probably wouldn't recognize her to even think to snap a picture; she's wildly famous in niche circles but a virtual unknown to everyone else—like TicTac influencers that all the kids know, but us old fuddyduddies couldn't pick out of a lineup."

Deandra didn't know if "TicTac" was a hub social site or if Heather also butchered mundane pop culture references.

"Despite her reputation," Heather continued, "she was able to drop everything and disappear into the ether." She frowned. "It's a shame, really. She had such a promising future. I do hope she's getting the help she needs."

The erratic behavior, if Ingrid truly had been Havoc's owner, could explain why such a rare—if not priceless—dragon ended up drugged and abandoned in a dumpster. It had been a crude hiding place at best, an inhumane method of disposal at worst. If Ingrid had suffered a mental collapse, Deandra would at least be able to offer up some sympathy.

She still wouldn't willingly give Havoc up—especially not to someone who had potentially dumped him like so much garbage. But sympathy could be mustered. A little.

Maybe.

"Where are, uh, some of the places she's been spotted? Ingrid, I mean," Deandra said, hoping she sounded casual enough.

The question seemed to throw Heather off. Perhaps because of all the things Heather had told them about the master blacksmith who might have been driven loopy under the weight of her own success, the locations of her sporadic sightings were the least interesting.

"Um ..." Heather said, brows furrowed for a moment as she regarded Deandra before her attention moved back to her screen. "Let's see ... she was supposedly seen in Kensey twice, Anderson in New York—which is where Grantham lives—Robinson last month ... and the last reported sighting, at least according to this was ..." Heather's eyes were nearly as wide now as they had been when she'd been wearing her steampunk spectacles. "The last sighting was right here in Axia roughly three months ago."

Wendy made a choking squeak noise that Deandra cut off by elbowing her cousin in the side. "Oh my!" Wendy said entirely too loudly. In a stilted tone, she added, "What a coinkidink."

Deandra, unable to help it, shot Wendy a *"really?"* look, because Deandra was fairly certain Wendy had never uttered the word "coinkidink" in her life.

Thankfully, Heather was more focused on the recent Ingrid Varros sighting than the cousins' dreadful acting skills. "And you said the coin you found was at the park, Deandra? The coin was in a terrible state, but I have no doubt that Ingrid would value it deeply. Not only does it bear her mark, but the metal it was forged from is fae in origin—and it's rumored she has a trunk full of such metals that she inherited from her great-grandfather. The metal alone would be considered priceless to many dwarves here." Expression pensive, Heather asked, "Do you think she might have run into foul play?"

Despite investigating an arson case recently—an arson case that doubled as a murder investigation, no less—Deandra had only briefly considered the possibility that something terrible had happened to Havoc's previous owner. She supposed it was just as likely that Ingrid had had every intention of returning for Havoc and had stashed him in the dumpster as a last-ditch effort to keep him safe—and then something nefarious had happened to her before she could make it back to Axia.

It still didn't explain how the coin ended up with Sunshine, of all creatures. While Deandra's nerves absolutely could not handle talking animals, this would all be so much easier if she could just *ask* Sunshine how she came into possession of the coin *and* why she'd been so adamant that Deandra take it.

Deandra asked, "Does the article say *where* in Axia she was seen? Or who reported it?"

"It says she was seen walking near an apartment complex on McClaren Way. I wonder if it was one of the complexes that was near the site of the fire last month ..."

Deandra had her elbow primed and ready to sink into Wendy's side again, but her cousin managed to keep her reaction in check. Havoc had been found in the dumpster in the parking lot of the art gallery that sat on the corner of McClaren and Purl. One apartment complex overlooked the parking lot on one side of the street, while another sat beside the building that had been burned to the ground via magical fire.

While Deandra knew that Ingrid had nothing to do with the fire—since the culprit had already been apprehended—it still put the dwarf at the scene of Havoc's abandonment. Who in Axia knew enough about the sordid details of master dwarven blacksmiths that they would have recognized Ingrid? And had Ingrid only been in Axia that one day, deposited Havoc, and then fled? Or had she been hiding out in Axia and slipped up somehow that day, resulting in her being spotted?

Deandra's eyes widened at a sudden realization. If Ingrid had either created the glamouring collar for Havoc herself, or had commissioned it, who was to say she couldn't have gotten something similar crafted for herself? The magic in Havoc's collar was powerful enough that it made him appear as a dire wolf to everyone but those in Havoc's inner circle. Would a less powerful glamouring talisman that adjusted only the hair color, or height, or gender of the wearer be enough to allow the famous Ingrid Varros to hide in plain sight? Had the glamouring magic on that talisman worn off the day she was last seen in Axia?

Perhaps Ingrid had strategically removed her talisman during her nomadic travels to purposefully create confusion about her whereabouts, resulting in a dozen random sightings across the hub system.

"*Deandra.*"

She snapped out of her spinning thoughts to find both Heather and Wendy staring at her. "Sorry. I was just remembering the fire. I was only a few blocks from it when the building went up in flames. There was this ... smell—like ammonia and burnt plastic. It just came back to me." She hoped her tone sounded apologetic.

Heather's expression softened. "Incredible how memory and scent are tied, isn't it?"

Deandra nodded, not trusting her mouth.

The pensive mood turned a tad awkward as they all struggled with what to say next. Heather returned to her task of getting rubbings from the coin. Deandra patiently waited for her to finish. Wendy's foot anxiously tapped the floor.

Once done, Heather rounded her desk and relinquished the coin to Deandra, her expression forlorn. The three women stood in a circle between the desk and office door.

"I'll let you know if I learn anything further. It's an intriguing magical mystery, to be sure," Heather said. "And perhaps you could consider donating the piece to a fae-themed museum? The idea of something so unique and beautiful being abandoned in a sticky cup holder or left on a nightstand hurts me to my very soul."

The dramatics would have been funny had Deandra not been sure that Heather meant that sincerely.

"I will," Deandra said. "And we'll let you know if we learn anything else, too."

Heather bobbed her head.

Finally finding her voice, Wendy said, "Try not to stay up all night poring over books on Dwarvish, okay?"

"No promises," Heather said. "It's a far better use of my time than binging *Hallow's Army*."

Deandra was half convinced Heather was getting the names wrong solely to troll Wendy.

"Blasphemy," Wendy said, then gave Heather a quick hug. "See you tomorrow. Thanks for the help."

"Anytime, ladies."

Deandra was about to head out the door after Wendy, who had just stepped into the store, when she thought of something she'd been meaning to ask since first visiting Heather. The coin was warm in Deandra's closed fist. She turned in the doorway. "Uh ... do you know why the coin hums when no one is touching it? It's not ... *alive*, alive, right? It's not humming in agony because it's lonely or something?"

Heather's smile was affectionate. "While the metal is living, it doesn't have a consciousness, so it doesn't *feel*. Not the way you're thinking, anyway. I do suspect that the coin is part of a set—a set of what, I'm not sure. My Dwarvish is ... well, rusty isn't a remotely accurate descriptor. But my best guess is that the coin's humming is due to it 'missing' its other half. When it's left on its own, it's humming for its ... purpose. If the rest of its set is found—whether that's one part or many—I believe the coin will go dormant."

Deandra mulled that over. "So it misses its family."

"If you wish to anthropomorphize it, then yes, exactly."

Deandra nodded. "Thanks a bunch, Heather. I really didn't know what to make of this. And I promise to research museums I can donate to."

Heather nodded tightly. Deandra wasn't sure if Heather's

pained expression spoke to her desire to keep the coin for herself, her worry that Deandra would defile the coin by doing something horrible to it—like turning it into jewelry—or her fear that Deandra didn't understand the coin's worth and would lose it.

Before Heather could change her mind about leaving it in Deandra's care, Deandra scurried out of the office.

# CHAPTER 6

When Deandra let herself into the passenger seat of Wendy's car parked in the back lot of Heather's Elixirs, she found her cousin tapping away on her phone screen. Deandra assumed she was texting her boyfriend, Nathan, though she hoped not—for Nathan's sake—given the deep crease of her brow.

Deandra waited patiently in silence for three seconds before saying, "Earth to—"

Wendy, without looking up from her phone, held up a finger to shush her. "Hold your horses. I'm working here."

Deandra rolled her eyes. The dramatic declaration meant Wendy was in a research wormhole, not in a digital argument with her new beau. She settled in to wait.

Mere seconds after Deandra finally cleared level 16 on Lollipop Jumble, Wendy shouted "Eureka!"

Deandra was so startled, she fumbled her phone, tossing it into the air before trying—and failing—to grab it before it thudded to the floorboard. Gusting a sigh, she shot an exasperated look at Wendy before rescuing her phone. "And what have you discovered?"

"So! I wanted to look up the supposed Ingrid sighting myself —to see if there were any clues about which apartment complex she'd been seen outside of. Asking too many questions about it would have made Heather even more suspicious than she already is."

There was a long dramatic pause.

Deandra tried to fight it, but she was weak—and Wendy knew it. "*And?*"

Wendy grinned. "There's a picture included in one of the articles of a lady mid-rant. It's not a very flattering picture. Makes her look like she's out of her gourd. The caption says, 'Axia resident who claims to have seen Ingrid Varros.' Thing is, I know the lady! Well, I don't *know* her, know her. She's been to the shop a few times. Heather is usually in her office or the classroom, so she doesn't interact with customers that often unless they have a specific request or complaint. I don't think she'd recognize her if she saw this picture.

"Anyway! I knew her first name was Petunia, but I didn't know her last name, so I was searching for her on socials. And I found her! Petunia Hartley. Her bio on Picayune says, 'Blacksmith trainee. Ingrid Varros IS ALIVE and TRAINING ME.' And there's a link to the article I just read. She has a pinned post from a few months ago about classes being held at In Flux We Trust, and she's there as an assistant three days a week."

Wendy's smile was so gleeful, it was bordering on manic.

"Does this mean what I think it does?" Deandra asked, defeated.

"Probably!" Wendy said, once again typing away at her phone. "I'm adding our names to the list for tomorrow."

"Tomorrow? The class hasn't already started? I thought you were going to suggest we have a stakeout in the parking lot and ambush Petunia when she leaves the class."

"It looks like it's drop-in," Wendy said, unfazed by Deandra's assumption that she had no qualms about harassing strangers. She scanned her phone's screen. "Above the sign-up form it says 'Due to low attendance in light of Ms. Hammerstrike's sudden departure—'"

Deandra held up a hand. "I'm sorry. Wait. *Hammerstrike?* That can't be a real name! That sounds like something off a fantasy name generator ..."

"That's what it says. In light of Hammerstrike's sudden departure, they're now offering classes for half price."

Convinced that Hammerstrike had to be a fake name, Deandra voiced one of the theories her wildly spinning mind had come up with in Heather's office. Namely that Ingrid Varros, a.k.a. Ms. Hammerstrike, a.k.a. Havoc's previous owner, was wearing something similar to Havoc's collar to glamour her appearance, allowing her to hide in plain sight.

Wendy apparently found this theory even more fascinating than her phone because she unceremoniously dropped it into her lap before turning in her seat to face Deandra. "If I hadn't already seen what Havoc's collar can do, I would have said that's impossible. I'm obviously not an expert on talismans like Heather is, but I know a lot. We don't sell *anything* in the store that has glamouring capabilities. Mundane colored contacts would do a better job at glamouring a person's appearance than anything we sell. Glamour magic isn't unheard of, but it's *very* rare. I mean, how scary would it be if it was common for people to change their faces at will? Ugh."

Creepy factor aside, Ingrid had either invested a lot of time or a lot of money into finding a way to disappear. Had it been a mental break—some overblown or outright erroneous sense of danger that had caused the master blacksmith to go on the lam?

Or had there been a *true* threat, and she'd dropped everything —including Havoc—out of self-preservation?

When Wendy had proposed the idea of crashing a beginner's blacksmithing class mere minutes ago, Deandra hadn't loved the idea. Sure, maybe Petunia really *had* spotted Ingrid in Axia, but the blacksmith was no doubt long gone by now. A very selfish part of Deandra wanted to let sleeping dogs lie. If Ingrid stayed gone— stayed away from Axia—it increased Deandra's chances of keeping Havoc for herself.

But that selfish part of her was being overridden by the fear that Ingrid could be in real trouble. She supposed she could voice her concerns to Officer Sutter, but what could the werecat do if Deandra had nothing but theories and guesses? Deandra wasn't sure how she'd explain to the officer why she was interested in Ingrid's whereabouts without revealing Havoc's possible connection to the blacksmith.

What if Officer Sutter wanted to take Havoc into custody until they figured out who legally had a claim to him? If Havoc ended up back in a system where someone like Ranger Vicks had access to him, Deandra was sure she'd never see him again.

She couldn't risk sharing his secret with anyone until she knew more.

Which was why, over the course of a few short minutes, she was now fully on board with Wendy's plan.

Deandra asked, "Is there a supply list?"

Wendy gave an excited squeal and clapped three times in rapid succession. "I know I've said it a million times, but I'm so glad you moved here! It felt like something vital had been missing from my life ... and now I know what it was."

Deandra was under no delusions that that something was her. "Sleuthing?"

"Sleuthing."

The class held at In Flux We Trust the following day began at five p.m., allowing Wendy enough time to come home from work and change before they headed to the shop. Deandra had taken Havoc on an hour-long walk earlier, and he was so wiped out that he didn't even stir from his position on the couch as the cousins got ready to leave. His front paws were flopped over his chest, and one would flick periodically in his sleep.

The shop happened to be a mere block away from Dr. Caddel's office. As Wendy drove past it, Deandra sank low in her seat for reasons even she couldn't understand. The lights were on in one of the windows, and only one car was in the lot. Maybe that was Cruz working after hours.

"You *do* like him, right?" Wendy asked, glancing over briefly. "Because this is avoiding-my-ex behavior and not I'm-hot-for-the-veterinarian behavior."

Deandra, face warm, sat up straighter in her seat. "Yes. I mean, I think so." She moaned pitifully. "See! I'm clearly not in any state to be dating anyone. He's got his stuff together, and I don't even know where most of my stuff is. Metaphorical stuff, I mean. I know where my *actual* stuff is. Though I swear a pair of shoes is missing, and I can't remember if I—"

"*Oh* my Goddess," Wendy said, exasperated. She pulled into a parking space in a nearly empty lot. She shut off the car and turned in her seat to fix Deandra with a *look*.

"*What?*"

"You do realize that you only get this weird about a guy when you like him, right? You get more self-deprecating than usual." Another *look* cut off Deandra's next protest before it could gain any steam. "You're scared. Starting something new is *usually* scary, no matter what it is. That's okay. From what I know of Dr. Caddel, he's good people. Give him a chance."

Deandra blew out a breath that puffed out her cheeks. "But he's so ... so ... you know. And I'm ..." She gestured at herself. "*This*. What if he's out of my league?"

"There's the self-deprecation. That's also the result of Mark treating you like arm candy instead of a partner." Wendy rolled her eyes. "Dr. Caddel went out of his way to help you and Havoc *several* times. He told you that the only payment he wants is lunch, which is code for wanting to spend time with you. Didn't you say he's obsessed with mythical animals to an almost embarrassing level, and that you being able to charm a dragon of all things practically made him swoon? Maybe he thinks *you're* out of *his* league."

Deandra couldn't imagine that was possible.

She also needed to talk about something else, so she cast her gaze out the window. They were in a parking lot outside a large warehouse-like building with three roll-up doors. The leftmost one belonged to a mechanic, while the other two were part of In Flux We Trust. Wendy was parked in front of the mechanic shop.

The building was covered in metal siding, and the middle roll-up door stood at half-mast, revealing an area cluttered with racks of tools, anvils on stands fashioned from tree trunks, and metal worktables. It gave off an intimidating medieval vibe, even from a distance. Deandra glanced down at her T-shirt, worn jeans, and even more worn tennis shoes. She'd convinced herself that everything on her body—skin included—would end up with burn holes by the end of the lesson, so she wore clothes she wasn't emotionally attached to. Burn holes in her unprotected skin would be a problem, though. Now she wished she'd worn something else; unfortunately her suit of armor was still at the dry cleaner.

Several feet away from the open roll-up door stood a grimy glass door that was presumably attached to an office or lobby. It swung open, the doorway filling with a lanky, wild-haired woman. She waved enthusiastically in their direction.

"That's Petunia. I don't know what her heritage is, but I think she's a quarter elf. Or was that nymph? She told me once. Anyway, she's got an iridescent sheen to her skin sometimes, almost like a pearl. And she's got pointed ears, but they aren't that much bigger than a human's ears," Wendy said. "By the way ... umm ... the sign-up form might have had a warning that said something like, 'Add your name to the list soon; we're filling up fast! We only allow ten students per class.'" She winced. "Then it said they had ten of ten spots available."

Deandra tore her gaze away from the still waving Petunia and cocked a brow at her cousin. "We're the only ones who signed up?"

Wendy flashed her a smile that was all teeth. "I know you're on board with the sleuthing, but I figured the social anxiety would get in the way if I told you you couldn't hide in the back of the classroom."

Deandra whimpered. This was the problem with having an extrovert for a best friend—they forced you into social situations for your own good.

"Remember," Wendy said gently, as if she were addressing a startled kitten, "you're here for the mystery. You're here for Havoc. And who knows! Maybe you're a prodigy blacksmith in disguise and you'll stroll out of here in an hour with a newly crafted dagger you can use to threaten your enemies!"

Deandra was not, in fact, a prodigy.

Well, she might have been, but this was *not* the day Deandra would discover any hidden talents. The "class" was so beginner level that the only tools Deandra and Wendy wielded were paper and pen as they took copious notes on blacksmithing history, terminology, and safety practices.

The only other person in the building was a slim, dark-skinned, bookish man in his sixties who looked more like a beatnik poet than a blacksmith. Did blacksmiths usually wear turtlenecks? Deandra guessed he was human.

When Wendy and Deandra had entered the small office where Petunia had been standing and waving, he had greeted the cousins from behind a glass-fronted counter whose shelves were lined with gleaming knives that had presumably been made in the shop.

After shaking their hands, he'd said, "I'm Glenn, the shop manager. I'm stuck doing boring inventory, but you'll be in good hands with Petunia. She's a rising star here at In Flux We Trust!"

Petunia had flushed almost as red as her wild hair, which was a bit of an unnerving sight with her pearlescent skin. She had the type of face that made age hard to parse; Deandra guessed some-where between twenty-five and forty. Her skin was unblemished, as if she'd never been a teenager who'd suffered through acne. Her green eyes were bright, and her smile was infectious.

Any excitement Deandra might have had for the class had died spectacularly in the first five minutes. Petunia's enthusiasm about explaining the name of the shop had been charming at first. Flux, she explained, was a substance such as borax used to create a low-temperature, glassy shield on a metal's surface to prevent oxida-tion. Then came a ten-minute deep dive on the various types of flux and why one was better than the other, especially when it came to metals with magical properties.

Deandra glanced over at Wendy's paper halfway through the lesson to find her sketching a rather gruesome depiction of Petunia fleeing a wild-eyed Wendy wielding a dagger.

"Gruesome" was a bit of an exaggeration, seeing as the drawing featured stick figures, but the message behind it was still crystal clear.

Perhaps it wasn't Ms. Hammerstrike's sudden departure that had caused attendance to plummet, but Petunia's teaching style. It would be hard to get students to keep coming back if they were bored to death. While Deandra was all for the motto "safety first," she didn't think it was necessary to give a lecture on the historical progression of materials used to craft goggles.

Glenn, apparently having finished doing inventory, had found a seat in the back of the classroom at some point, presumably to watch his rising star in action. The faint snore issuing from behind Deandra now suggested that even Glenn found the lecture lacking.

For whatever reason, Petunia had rolled out a chalkboard and had been drawing surprisingly detailed and wholly unnecessary pictures to accompany her lesson. Her back had been to her audience for the better part of twenty minutes.

When she concluded the class with, "Next week, we'll begin with a fascinating tale about the history of charcoal!"

Deandra whooped and clapped loudly, both to distract Petunia from the state of her students, and to wake *up* said students. Wendy's chin slipped off her propped-up fist at the sudden commotion, and she nearly toppled out of her chair. "Bravo!" Deandra said, keeping Petunia's attention on her while Wendy hastily wiped drool from the corner of her mouth.

"Well done!" came Glenn's semi-slurred praise from behind Deandra. "Mag-uhh-nificent." A few moments later, Glenn had joined Petunia in front of the room, hands held behind his back as he took in the details on the chalkboard. In a whisper that carried easily given how empty the place was, he asked, "You, uh, didn't even light the forge, did you?"

Petunia's shoulders stiffened. "People must understand the history before they can appreciate the art."

"And while that is a commendable stance, truly, the history of the ball-peen hammer is unlikely to make people part with their money."

Wendy and Deandra quickly looked at each other and then

back at their notes, the ceiling, the back wall—anywhere but at Petunia and Glenn. It was as if they'd stumbled into the middle of a lover's spat, though Petunia was half his age, and there didn't appear to be romantic interest complicating the situation. It was more like an opinionated employee who'd grown too comfortable with her boss, blurring the lines of who held the authority.

Petunia looked as if Glenn's declaration about the ball-peen hammer had hit her with all the force of the tool itself. Though she was still whispering furiously, her tone rose a bit in volume. "I'm here to train the next generation of blacksmiths. Do you want the art—much like its storied history—to be lost to the annals of time?"

A flicker of white in Deandra's periphery caught her eye, and she glanced over. Wendy had slid her stick-figure-massacre masterpiece closer to her, and in the corner, she'd written a note.

*I forgot to mention Petunia is <u>very</u> dramatic.*

Deandra narrowly managed to turn her laughter into a choked cough.

The bickering pair didn't seem to notice.

Glenn, in a slightly louder tone, said, "I'm grateful for how you stepped in when Ms. Hammerstrike—"

Petunia petulantly stomped her foot. "Ingrid Varros." She jabbed a finger in the man's face. "Treat her name with the respect it deserves!"

Deandra couldn't tell if Glenn was more put out by the disrespect or by what was clearly a well-worn argument.

"You were *not* being trained by a master blacksmith, Petunia!" Glenn snapped. "Your eyes deceived you. I know you want it to be true. You're a passionate young lady. I respect that deeply about you. But this foolishness needs to stop!" Holding his clenched fists by his sides, he straightened his shoulders. He had a good four inches on her in height, and yet it was as if Petunia was looking down on *him*. "I'm ... I've actually ... that is to say, I'm going to begin holding interviews this coming week for Ms. Hammerstrike's replacement."

Petunia, hand to chest, stumbled back a step, these words hitting even harder than Glenn's disparaging remarks about the ball-peen hammer. "You mean you're replacing *me*."

"You were a temporary placeholder when Ms. Hammerstrike—"

"Varros! How can you *possibly* take a name like Hammerstrike seriously? A fantasy name generator could do better."

"That's what *I* said!"

Deandra winced when she realized she'd said that out loud, and three sets of eyes swiveled her way.

Glenn awkwardly cleared his throat, and Petunia rolled her shoulders, as if they'd both just remembered they weren't alone, embarrassed their argument had had an audience.

Petunia ineffectively smoothed a hand over her wild mop of hair. "We'll discuss this later. I ... I have to go."

Eyes limned with silver, Petunia abruptly left.

Wendy quickly shoved her chair back. "Thanks so much for the hospitality, Glenn!"

Deandra scrambled to her feet as well. "Yes, thank you!"

The cousins hurried for the door. Deandra quickly doubled back to collect their notes, if only to keep Glenn from seeing Wendy's stick-figure slaughter and calling the cops.

She darted out the door.

# CHAPTER 7

When Deandra made it into the parking lot, she easily spotted Wendy and Petunia. They stood outside the closed mechanic shop near Wendy's car. Well, Wendy was doing the lion's share of the standing, as Petunia was leaning against her, openly sobbing. The woman's weeping sounded vaguely reminiscent of a wounded cat.

Deandra considered strolling past the emotional display and venturing home on foot to avoid ... all of this.

Steeling herself, she slowly approached the pair. From what Deandra could make out between gasping breaths, Petunia felt "a level of betrayal" she hadn't experienced since "Agnes stole her pig."

Deandra was unclear if the pig had been a pet or if this was an unearthed trauma from when Petunia was six and her favorite stuffed animal had been pilfered by a villainous sibling. Deandra wasn't going to ask for clarification.

When there was a blissful lull in the caterwauling, Wendy quickly asked, "Is teaching your passion, or is it blacksmithery?"

Wendy had been gently petting the woman's head as if she really were a cat that needed soothing, and her hand fell away now as Petunia removed her head from Wendy's shoulder.

After a pronounced sniff and a great shuddering breath, Petunia said, "Blacksmithery isn't a word."

Deandra, upon seeing Wendy's pinched expression, cut in before she could say something snarky and set Petunia off again. "I heard you say *Ingrid Varros* was the teacher before you. You didn't mean *the* Ingrid Varros, did you?"

Deandra found that having a set task kept her introverted soul from withering and dying when she needed to chat up strangers. When she was a barista, having a counter between her and the customers worked as a barrier, giving her a role to play. Sleuthing gave her conversation topics.

If the task had been to make small talk with randos at a party, Deandra would have rather slithered under her bed.

Petunia's bloodshot eyes widened. "You know who she is?"

Deandra quickly spewed all the facts she knew about Ingrid and hoped Petunia couldn't tell this knowledge was less than twenty-four hours old. "To be honest, I wanted to take the class here in part because there's a rumor you actually saw Ingrid in Axia. Did she ..." Deandra took a step closer and lowered her voice to a conspiratorial whisper. "Did she reveal her true identity to you? We think she might be glamouring her appearance, but everyone thinks we're crazy. I mean, it's not like glamour magic is common."

Petunia bounced on the balls of her feet and nodded vigorously. "Yes! Oh my Goddess! This is what I've been trying to tell people, and no one will believe me!"

Wendy spoke up. "Did she show you what she's been using to glamour herself? She must really trust you!"

Petunia's beaming smile slipped a bit. "I saw her true face by accident. She was in the shop after hours. I'd left earlier in the day but came back because I forgot my phone. When I let myself in, she was talking to someone, so she didn't hear me come in. I guess she forgot I had a key. Glenn was on vacation for the week, so she didn't expect anyone to show up. There was a metal bracelet on one of the tables—really pretty blueish-colored metal. I think it was dwarven aureate! She turned around when I was examining the bracelet. She ... she wasn't happy. Yelled at me *a lot*. I started crying—partly because she can be *really* mean, and partly because *oh my Goddess*, it was Ingrid-*freaking*-Varros, you know?"

Wendy and Deandra bobbed their heads.

Petunia gusted a world-weary sigh. "She threatened me. She said if I told anyone who she really was, she'd tell Glenn she saw me stealing from the till and get me fired. Which I absolutely *never* did! Glenn is like an uncle to me. I'd never steal from him."

After a long pause, Deandra asked, "So, uh, how did you end up in the *Axian Gazette* saying you saw Ingrid near the apartment complex where that building burned down last month?"

Petunia's nose wrinkled, and the pointed tips of her pearlescent ears went pink. "Things between me and Ingrid got ... contentious after I discovered her identity. She said staying hidden was hard for her, even though she had that bracelet. Our arrangement was that she'd train me in blacksmithing, and in exchange, I'd help her out here and there so she could limit how often she was in public.

"At first it was a quick run to a convenience store. Then it was grocery shopping once a week. Then it was taking her car to the mechanic. And making appointments for her. And supply runs—which usually meant I had to go into other hubs for obscure items. I was getting really great training from her—I mean *great* training—but she was starting to take advantage of how generous I am. It was a rough few months. It's lucky that I'm such a natural-born talent who learns quickly; otherwise, our arrangement would have been very one-sided."

There was too much to unpack there, so Deandra preemptively elbowed Wendy in the side to keep her from commenting.

"The week of that fire," Petunia continued, "Ingrid was acting very erratic. Even more than usual, I mean. A little eccentricity goes hand in hand with genius. I should know. But she was, I don't know ... paranoid. She told me she had a very important task to take care of, and that if the task went sideways, she might have to leave Axia for a while. She wouldn't tell me what was going on. But she *did* tell me that if things went bad, someone might come looking for her, and that I had to keep her secrets at all costs or she'd 'ruin' me. Three days before the fire, Glenn called me into the office and handed me a note that *Ms. Hammerstrike* left on his desk."

Wendy let the silence stretch for roughly zero point four seconds. "What did it say?"

Petunia's eyes welled up again. "The note said that I was very talented, but my misguided delusion that she was actually Ingrid Varros or someone connected to her, and my relentless attempts to *weave myself into the very fabric of her everyday life,* had become so suffocating that she was leaving Axia to escape me. She said she didn't think I needed to be fired, but I probably needed medical attention to treat my unhealthy fixation."

Wendy winced. "Yikes."

"Double yikes," Deandra added.

Petunia's fists were clenched by her sides, her jaw tight.

Deandra wasn't sure if she was going to start crying again or if she wanted to punch something. Maybe both.

"She made my life miserable for months, but she ensured I kept taking the abuse because I learned more from her in those few months than I'd learned in years. Now I get a new custom order for knives at least once a week. She didn't only teach me about bladesmithing; she taught me invaluable marketing lessons, too. I owe much of my current success to her.

"But she's also a *monster*! Glenn almost *did* fire me. Ingrid abruptly leaving really put him in a bind. He ended up offering partial refunds to dozens of people who had signed up for several of her courses that were supposed to run for a full year. We desperately need a power hammer, and those funds would have paid for it. We might not be able to purchase it until next year now.

"Ingrid was offering private classes too, and Glenn was getting a portion of the fee since Ingrid was renting out a section of In Flux We Trust to conduct the lessons. All of that revenue was gone. He truly thought I'd run her out of town. Sometimes I wonder if he still thinks that."

"How did you convince him you didn't?" Deandra asked.

Petunia gusted a sigh. "I didn't, really. Once he got over the shock of it, I think he came to his senses. He'd only known *Ms. Hammerstrike* for a handful of months, and he'd known me for years. He was blinded by how much business improved when she joined the shop. But if Ingrid truly had been put off by my supposed obsession, why didn't she just talk to him about it? Leaving with no warning and telling him in a note that he wouldn't find until she was long gone was a crappy move, even if she *was* trying to escape me. She disconnected her phone number, too, so he couldn't even call her to talk about it."

The more Deandra heard about Ingrid Varros, the less she knew what to make of her.

With an air of caution, Wendy said, "Doesn't sound like he believes Ms. Hammerstrike and Ingrid are the same person."

Petunia gave one sharp shake of her head. "He's been very selective about which parts of the story he believes. The esteemed Ingrid Varros hiding right under our noses was too much for him to accept. Maybe because it would make him feel foolish. I don't know. But that's our biggest point of contention lately. I voiced my concern that 'Hammerstrike' was an alias long before I caught Ingrid without her bracelet. I suspect Glenn is kicking himself for not trusting my intuition from the start—and some part of him is offended that *the* Ingrid Varros decided to take *me* under her wing and not him."

This time Wendy elbowed Deandra in the side, keeping her from saying that she suspected Ingrid knew she'd have a better chance at manipulating Petunia than Glenn. Petunia's ego was both malleable *and* overinflated. Ingrid probably figured out that she could get away with a lot with the aid of strategically placed compliments.

Deandra asked, "So did you *actually* see Ingrid near that apartment building? Did she come back to Axia after she left without warning?"

Nodding vigorously, Petunia said, "I saw her a day before the fire. She was using a different glamouring device—one that didn't alter her height or her voice. I'd recognize that voice anywhere. I heard her yelling at a pair of kids. I guess they ran past her on the sidewalk, and one bumped into her and almost made her drop her coffee. One kid got so upset, he was bawling his eyes out. He might have been around seven; hard to tell with imps—especially the midnight ones."

Deandra shot a wide-eyed look at Wendy, silently asking for clarification.

"Horned fae," Wendy said in a stage whisper. "The midnight ones have dark blue skin."

Deandra remembered seeing a pair of blue-skinned beings on her first day in Axia.

Undeterred by the interruption, Petunia continued. "The parents of the imps had been walking farther back and rushed to catch up when Ingrid started screaming at them. Then she and *the parents* got into a shouting match. Midnight imps, if they have magic at all, usually wield ice. The ticked-off lady imp blasted Ingrid with a mini blizzard that either knocked her glamouring talisman clean off, or neutralized it, because she was fully ... *her*. A crowd had formed by then, but no one recognized her but me. She panicked when she realized her glamour was gone, and then she saw me watching her from across the street. She pointed at me, drew a line across her neck with a finger, then took off down the sidewalk, slamming into people as she went.

"A reporter from the *Gazette* just happened to be inside the art gallery during all this but only caught the tail end of the commotion when the imp parents got involved. He didn't recognize Ingrid, either, but he saw the death glare Ingrid shot at me, so he asked me what was going on. So ..." Petunia hiked her chin in the air, defiant. "I told him the lady fleeing the scene was *the* Ingrid Varros and that she'd been hiding in Axia for months. I told him all kinds of things, honestly, but somehow the spin of the article was that I was touched in the head and just another crackpot in a long string of crackpots who have claimed to see Ingrid in various hubs. Instead of it being an article about my harrowing experience with that monstrous yet brilliant woman, he turned it into a story about how people are obsessed with status and fame, riding on the coattails of others or whatever, instead of chasing their own successes. Offensive.

"If he'd *bothered* to listen, he'd know I'm successful in my own right! I was giving him the scoop of a lifetime, and here he was with his purple prose, trying to win a Yari with his hot take on the culture of celebrity." She blew a raspberry. "And he besmirched my sanity while doing it!"

Deandra idly wondered if a Yari was the hub system's equivalent of a Pulitzer. She also decided she never wanted to be in a room with Petunia and Ingrid at the same time. The pairing sounded exhausting at best and toxic at worst.

Wendy asked, "You weren't worried Ingrid was going to see the article and retaliate?"

Petunia's lips tightened into a thin line for a moment before she spoke, clearly lying through her teeth. "I'm not scared of Ingrid. She did her worst already, and in spite of her efforts to destroy my career, now I've taken her place at In Flux We Trust. I rose to the occasion; I wasn't felled by it."

Instead of elbowing each other, Deandra and Wendy exchanged quick glances, silently telling the other not to remind Petunia that Glenn was actively looking for her replacement.

"So you haven't seen Ingrid since the day before the fire?" Deandra asked. "Do you think she could still be in town, but is glamouring herself again?"

"My guess is she donned another disguise to help her clean up some loose ends for a couple of days, but she's long gone now," Petunia said. "Being a horrible person aside, she had to have been spooked—and spooked *bad*—to give up her life the first time. Something or someone must have spooked her again while she was in Axia for her to just pick up and leave like that. The look on her face when I caught her without her glamour was pure fear—as if I'd walked up to her pointing a loaded gun. Me learning her identity wasn't enough to totally freak her out; she would have left immediately after I found out. But she stuck around for months after that."

"And you have no idea what scared her into picking up and leaving again?" Deandra asked.

Petunia eyed her curiously, as if she was just now starting to wonder why Deandra and Wendy were this invested in the puzzle that was Ingrid Varros.

Deandra quickly appealed to vanity. "I can't believe you don't have at least a *couple* of theories. She must have trusted you more than she trusted anyone else in Axia. I mean, she's been on the run for months, you discovered her secret, and not only did she *not* flee town, she offered to train you. She either saw you as a possible confidant or as a formidable adversary who needed to be neutralized."

That last, dramatic line had been pulled almost verbatim from the mouth of Mikayla Grassly. The stifled squawk from her cousin said Wendy recognized it. Deandra really hoped Petunia wasn't a die-hard *Faet of the Heart* fan.

Thankfully, Petunia puffed up at the praise. Deandra really *did* think it was possible Ingrid had confided in Petunia, even if indirectly, during her months of using the woman as a glorified errand girl. She didn't think Ingrid would have divulged something so scandalous as being the owner of a thought-to-be-extinct dragon. But Deandra also doubted there were too many other people in Axia who'd interacted with Ms. Hammerstrike and known she was actually the infamous Ingrid Varros. As dramatic and prone to delusions of grandeur as Petunia was, Deandra sensed an air of insightfulness.

"I'd only been inside her apartment a couple of times," Petunia said. "She mostly had me drop off supplies on her porch. And if I was going to take her to an appointment, she met me at the curb like I was her taxi driver. But her place was beyond minimalist—mattress on the floor, nothing hanging on the walls, clothes in hampers and open suitcases, no shelves or knickknacks. She kept all her blacksmithing tools in a giant trunk—like a treasure chest. I'm sure that thing was either a beloved family heirloom or was super expensive. It was the only high-quality thing she seemed to own. She lived like she was always two seconds from needing to pack up and go.

"The day after she left that note for Glenn, I went to her studio apartment, ready to confront her. The blinds on her unit were open. She never left them open. I practically crawled into the hedge under the window to look in. The room was cleared out ... all except for the bare mattress and that dang treasure chest. Why would she leave *that* behind? She'd lugged that thing to Axia, after all. But something obviously scared her so bad that she left her one prized possession." Her expression was a bit sad, clearly worried about Ingrid, even if their relationship had been messy. "It makes me sick that I can't get in there to take whatever's in that trunk. If she doesn't want it, ownership should revert to me as her apprentice. But the nasty apartment manager won't let me in! He said he'll only let in *actual prospective renters*."

Deandra asked, "Wouldn't the trunk be considered abandoned property? Maybe you just have to wait for him to throw it out."

Petunia shook her head. "I asked him that, too. He said it's such a unique piece, he's going to keep it in there, get a few more pieces from the thrift shop, and jack up the rent on the unit because now it's 'furnished.'" She added air quotes, punctuated by an eye roll. Then her shoulders slumped. "That's probably my fault. If I had just left well enough alone, he *might* have tossed it. I mentioned how priceless it was too many times, and I watched in real time as the lightbulb went off in his head and dollar signs practically flashed in his eyes."

"What if you offered to buy it from him?" Wendy asked.

"He'd quote me something ludicrous. I guess that's my fault, too." Petunia crossed her arms. "I think he might have caught me in the bushes the day I was peeking in Ingrid's window. I've tried a bunch of different stories with him—that I'm her best friend, that she left the trunk for me, that she called me the other day and wanted me to collect the trunk for her, since she forgot it. He's too greedy to give it up now. Someone is going to rent that apartment, take that trunk—and *my* inheritance—and probably sell it on some auction site on Forage for a pretty penny. I'll never get to see what's in there. Assuming the greedy little monster hasn't already figured out how to open it. I highly doubt he did, though. He's not a mundane, but he might as well be; he's totally useless." Her gaze flicked between Deandra and Wendy. "No offense," she added without a hint of remorse.

Deandra didn't find the term offensive. Plus, it wasn't as if Petunia was that far from mundane herself. She was only a quarter elf or nymph—her ancestry only contributing to her appearance.

Deandra was desperately curious to know what was in this trunk now—assuming there was anything left at all. Maybe Ingrid had taken her tools and supplies and left the bulky thing behind in her haste to get away.

And yet. She'd clearly either been in Axia again after her abrupt departure from In Flux We Trust, or she'd been hiding while glamoured, so why hadn't she circled back for one of the few valuable pieces of furniture she owned? Heather had said, *"Not only does the coin bear her mark, but the metal it was forged from is fae in origin—and it's rumored she has a trunk full of such metals that she inherited from her great-grandfather."*

Deandra's thoughts strayed back to Havoc. Had Ingrid cut ties with him, just like she'd cut ties with everything else? Had she decided he, much like the trunk, was too much of a hindrance? Perhaps she'd returned to Axia merely to knock Havoc out with a powerful controlled substance and then had left him in a dumpster so that when he woke up in a landfill, he'd be someone else's problem.

It wasn't as if abandoning pets in cruel ways wasn't common in the mundane world, but Deandra supposed she'd hoped that Axia was different. People chained unwanted pets to fences at parks. They moved homes and left their animals behind. Some even dumped them out of moving cars on the highway.

She hoped she'd never meet Ingrid Varros, as she was sure to say or do something she'd later regret.

"You probably don't believe me when I use the word inheritance," Petunia said, snapping Deandra out of a mental scenario that was ten times more gruesome than Wendy's stick-figure drawings. Petunia looked unsure of herself for a moment, as if debating whether she wanted to say this next part out loud. "Ingrid left me an envelope under my welcome mat a couple of days *after* the fire.

Inside was a note that said 'I've left something for you at my apartment. Use this to gain entry. If you're as smart as I think you are, you'll figure it out.' There wasn't a key or anything, though. Just a crusty, humming coin."

Deandra and Wendy both gasped, telegraphing their shock with all the subtlety of a ninja festooned with cowbells.

Luckily for them, Petunia thrived on dramatics like most people thrived on oxygen. "Right? So random. But I was up for the challenge. Plus some part of me wondered if she was disguised and watching me, waiting to see if I could pass her test. I thought maybe she'd loop me into her life in a more meaningful way if I could decode her clues. Anyway, I do my best thinking while I'm on the move, so I took a walk in Oracle Park, turning that coin over and over in my hand. You won't believe what happened while I was there!"

Oh, but Deandra would.

Petunia told them that she'd been ambushed by an unhinged fire newt. Sunshine, from the sound of it, had launched out of a tree onto Petunia's shoulder. Pandemonium had ensued, as one might expect.

"This is going to sound crazy, but when the newt first attacked me, I thought it was a run-of-the-mill attack by a rabid animal, you know?" Petunia asked. "I don't think it really had an agenda other than sating its boredom, bloodlust, or both. But at some point during the vicious assault, it noticed the coin in my hand. It went absolutely still. It stared at the coin as if it were a long-lost friend. I tried to appeal to it, holding my hand open with the coin lying on my palm so the newt could see it better. After a few long seconds, the newt looked at me. I mean *really* looked at me.

"It started hissing up a storm, but it almost seemed like it was trying to talk to me. When I told it that the coin was a gift from Ingrid Varros, the newt went berserk. It was in my hair, then on my arm, then hissing in my ear. I pulled the demon off me and chucked it like a football, then ran in the opposite direction. It chased me! Caught up faster than should have been possible, too. The newt managed to trip me. I went down hard. My purse fell off my shoulder, and the coin was knocked out of my hand.

"By the time I got to my feet, the note from Ingrid that was in my purse *and* the coin were gone. I can't report the coin missing. How in *all the realms* am I supposed to explain the incident to the werecats? *Hi, an infamous dwarf who has been in town for months but glamoured to look like someone else left me a magical coin. She left town without a trace—at least I think so. Who can say? I need the magical coin to gain access to something in her vacated apartment. No, I'm not related to her. No, I have no proof of any of this. Can you let me in anyway?*" She gusted a deep sigh.

Not only did Deandra believe every word of Petunia's loopy story, the magical coin in question was burning a hole in her pocket. She'd tried to leave it behind today, but the thing had taken to humming forlornly if it wasn't either on Deandra's person or within eyesight—or whatever the coin equivalent to eyesight was, anyway. It was one of those too-weird Axia things that were better left not thought about too hard lest Deandra's brain explode.

The problem now was, Deandra felt like she couldn't return the coin to Petunia until she knew more. What if there was information in that trunk about Havoc? Deandra would fight tooth and nail to keep him rather than returning him to the likes of Ingrid Varros, but what if one or both of Havoc's parents were somehow alive? Details about *multiple* thought-to-be-extinct dragons would be the kind of thing someone would keep under lock and key, right? If his parents were still alive, he'd belong with them above all else. Didn't she owe it to Havoc to do her due diligence to make sure he had a good life, despite its tumultuous beginning?

Deandra supposed, too, that Ingrid's whereabouts could possibly be surmised from the contents of that trunk. As much as Deandra didn't want to interact with her, the dwarf was the one who knew the most about Havoc. What if there was some vital piece of information—like about his health—that Deandra needed to know?

She warred with the two choices: keep the coin a secret from Petunia until she'd learned all she could, or hand the coin to Petunia, wish her luck, and wash her hands of the whole messy affair.

She recalled the way Sunshine had touched her own face before pressing her little hand to the coin. It sounded like Sunshine had done everything she could to get the coin *away* from Petunia, yet she'd willingly given it to Deandra. So it wasn't the coin itself that Sunshine coveted ...

She stilled as a thought struck her.

Was it possible that Sunshine was connected to Ingrid's menagerie of fire-aligned animals, just as Deandra suspected Havoc was? Perhaps Sunshine had gone "berserk" when she'd seen the coin in Petunia's hand and heard Ingrid's name because she'd recognized both. Deandra knew nothing of Sunshine's history other than who had owned her a month or so ago, but she had a suspicion that Sunshine had been purchased from the Mythic Pet Kitchen, the pet store in town that catered exclusively to exotic and mythical pets.

"Earth to Deandra!"

She flinched and found Petunia and Wendy staring at her expectantly. "Sorry. Uhh ... did you ask me something?"

"You're a little scatterbrained, aren't you?" Petunia asked.

Deandra leveled her with a flat stare.

"*Petunia here,*" Wendy said in an overly sweet tone, clearly trying to defuse any mounting hostility, "was just saying how rude Archibald Livingstone—the apartment manager—is and how terrible it is that he's no longer even taking her phone calls."

"Too bad you don't have Ingrid's glamouring bracelet," Deandra mused. "You could assume her fake identity and stroll right in there."

A small, borderline creepy smile graced Petunia's face. "I'm working on that. All I need is another ten grand, and the glamourer I found on the arcane web will help me."

"Ten *grand*?" Deandra asked, bewildered. "I don't know if—"

Petunia held up a hand to quiet her. "If I keep taking on custom orders, I'll have the funds I need in two weeks. The nasty reviews I keep posting about the pixie problem plaguing McClaren Oaks should buy me the time I need. And if worse comes to worst, I'll either kidnap several pixies or pay them to make the reviews true."

Wendy's mouth dropped open.

Deandra honestly didn't know how to respond. Petunia was such a confusing mess of sympathetic, unbalanced, and unsettling.

The cousins' befuddlement apparently gave Petunia the out she needed.

"It's been lovely chatting, ladies. I feel much better. And you've reminded me I need to send the glamourer a check-in message." With a salute, Petunia turned on her heel and headed back toward the blacksmith shop. Instead of going inside, though, Petunia stopped at a row of bike racks and proceeded to pull the lone bicycle free.

Deandra and Wendy didn't say anything as they watched Petunia pedal across the parking lot, giving a little trill of her bike bell before easing out onto the road and riding out of view.

"*Sooo*," Wendy finally said, dragging out the word. "She's a lot."

Deandra snorted. Her mirth quickly faded, though, as she wondered if she needed to call Officer Sutter to warn her about Petunia in general. If nothing else, Deandra considered dropping by the hedge where the Clarion clan lived to warn them that there was yet another Axian resident who might attempt to use pixies in their criminal exploits.

Wendy cut into her musings. "What's on the agenda tomorrow in light of this new intel? To give Archibald Livingstone a shakedown?"

"Do you even know what it *means* to give someone a shakedown?" Deandra asked, arms crossed.

"No clue. But it sounds cool, doesn't it?"

"What if, instead of a shakedown, we try to get an appointment to see the apartment?" Deandra asked. "Archibald is more likely to answer a few of our overly nosy questions if we're there legally. I'd rather not have to add breaking and entering to my list of new skills."

"I'm surprised Petunia didn't try that already. If she's seriously considering pixienapping, why not just chuck a brick through a window and *really* embrace the dark side?"

Deandra frowned. "Do we need to go warn the pixies?"

"Which ones? There are thousands of them here. We can't exactly warn all of them. Plus, they can take care of themselves better than you think. Those little buggers are *super* bitey. And even though Petunia is kinda bonkers, she's not exactly a criminal mastermind. I have a feeling if any of them sense Petunia's menacing aura coming, they'll chase her away like a swarm of airborne piranhas."

Deandra stared at her cousin for several long seconds. "You truly don't know what's weird anymore, do you? Therefore, I will be the voice of reason: We're not going to *shake down* Archibald Livingstone. We'll make a *legal* appointment and we will ask questions like good old-fashioned sleuths. Because *we* aren't criminal masterminds either."

"Oh, fine," Wendy said, turning toward her car. "But I still think a shakedown sounds like more fun."

# CHAPTER 8

At four-fifteen the next afternoon, Deandra and Wendy stood outside the McClaren Oaks apartment complex. The building had once been a borderline seedy motel, but it had been refurbished to within an inch of its life. The fact that all the doors faced the parking lot still gave it a "no one stays here for long" vibe, though. Maybe that was why Ingrid Varros had chosen it.

According to the website, the walls between several rooms had been knocked out, turning the once forty-five-room motel into an apartment complex with sixteen one-bedroom units, three two-bedroom units, and four studios. Ingrid had been renting out one of the studios.

Deandra had called the apartment complex this morning, as she didn't trust Wendy with the task. What if she'd tried to give Archibald Livingstone a *verbal* shakedown, and then he also forbade *them* from ever entering the apartment?

Havoc sat dutifully by Deandra's feet, though he kept snapping at the air, pestered as he was by an insistent fly. Deandra silently willed her dragon not to get so annoyed with the insect that he launched a small fireball to incinerate it. While McClaren Oaks was a pet-friendly apartment complex, Deandra figured Archibald Livingstone might be less inclined to approve of Havoc if he gave off the impression he was capable of setting the building on fire.

Deandra was also curious whether Archibald would recognize Havoc's dire wolf glamour, as Ingrid might have been keeping him at the apartment with her.

The image Deandra had conjured of the apartment manager was admittedly shaped by mundane television shows and movies, but she'd expected a sweaty man in a stained white tank top and a bad combover. What she got was an avian shifter whose distant ancestors must have been parrots or some equally colorful bird.

All Petunia had said about him was, "He's not a mundane, but he might as well be."

Deandra would beg to differ. Clearly Petunia had an even looser hold on the concept of what constituted normal for a mundane than Wendy did.

Even though Deandra was still not remotely an expert on the dozens of species that called Axia home, avian shifters were one of the few she was able to identify immediately. The first avian she'd met was Allegra from the Welcome Center. The woman had abruptly shifted from human to ostrich-sized swan and back again.

If that hadn't been alarming on its own, while in human form, Allegra never quite looked "right." Her neck was too long, her eyes were spaced too far apart, and her hair was made of feathers.

Deandra's shock at Allegra's incongruous features hadn't upset the woman. *"I am well aware that an avian shifter's face, to a human, looks like chaos,"* she'd said.

Archibald Livingstone's features weren't nearly as chaotic, but his skin was mint green, and his hair was a riot of colorful feathers that hung past his ears. From far away, it looked like a shaggy seventies-style hairstyle that boasted at least six colors. Up close, especially when a breeze hit it just right, the feathers fluttered. He had a long and lean body, and when paired with the sharp slate-gray suit he wore, he looked like he'd be right at home among the business class in a bustling city like New York.

The rainbow-feather hair was ... distracting, though. Was it possible to *dye* feathers? If one plucked the feathers out, would they grow back?

Deandra winced when she got an elbow to the side. She snapped out of her gawking and coughed awkwardly. "Sorry," she muttered, even though she wasn't sure what, specifically, she was apologizing for. Either way, she was sure it was warranted.

When Deandra focused on the bird shifter, Archibald, unlike Allegra, was *not* amused by Deandra's shock. He looked down his beak-like nose at her. "New to the hub system, are you? Only *mundanes* are this rude."

This was the first time she'd heard the word "mundane" sound like a slur, and Deandra's hackles rose.

Wendy jumped in before Deandra could get them banned without even stepping foot inside Ingrid's old apartment. "Ha ha!" Wendy said, taking on her atrocious actress voice. "Oh, don't mind Dee here. Her ex was an avian shifter, and he looked a lot like you. He was killed in a boating accident a few months ago. Seeing you was probably like seeing a ghost!"

Deandra didn't have to fake tears for her newly deceased imaginary avian boyfriend, as she was so startled by the nonsense that had just spewed from Wendy's mouth, she spluttered a laugh so abrupt it triggered a coughing fit. Her eyes welled. Deandra covered her face with her hands as she did her best to morph the cough into some approximation of sobs. Wendy patted her back comfortingly.

Havoc chirped, as if asking if she were okay. He rubbed his muzzle against her knee. Deandra lowered one hand from her face so she could give him a scratch behind an ear. "I'm okay," she croaked, then loudly cleared her throat, which caused another coughing fit. She pounded her free hand against her chest. "Wendy just surprised me by, uhh, sharing my secret pain with a stranger."

Havoc's head whipped toward Wendy, then he growled at her.

Wendy threw her hands up in innocence. "She needs to talk about Magnus Barbery, or she'll never be able to move past it!"

Deandra was overcome by another coughing fit.

Havoc peeped angrily.

Archibald Livingstone hmmed. "It's unconventional for avians to stray outside their species ... but if you were able to woo a Barbery, *and* you've got the mental fortitude to train a dire wolf—and a puppy at that!—I must say I'm starting to see the appeal. I already find you *very* fetching visually, which is saying a lot for me, as your limbs are entirely too short to be conventionally attractive."

Reluctantly, Deandra glanced at the avian shifter. She swallowed hard when she saw the look on his incongruous face.

"Thank you?" she ventured.

He gave her an elevator scan. "If I wasn't ... a *purist*, I might be so inclined to partake in wooing you myself. Once you were past your grief, anyway."

His delivery of "purist" was unconvincing.

Oh, heaven help her.

No, heaven help *Wendy*, because Deandra was going to *strangle* her later.

"Ha ha!" Wendy fake-laughed again. "Well, if we get to move in here, you'll be able to see each other more often."

Deandra shot her a *look* then. Given the startling red hue of Wendy's face, Wendy clearly knew she'd taken this improv session entirely too far, but the train was already off the tracks, and there was no stopping it.

"I guess we should get this tour started then, shouldn't we?" Archibald asked. "You wanted to see both a two-bedroom and a studio, yes?"

Deandra nodded, having gotten her coughing-induced tears under control. "It would be a tight fit for two people in a studio—especially with a growing dire wolf—but it's more in line with our budget."

"The previous tenant of the studio had a mangy kitten for a pet. It'll be nice to have a big, strong guard dog on the premises."

Havoc squared his feet and puffed up his chest, chirping once, as if to say he was up for the job. Deandra meanwhile wondered if the mangy kitten Archibald mentioned had been an alternate glamour for Havoc or if Ingrid had also been in possession of a fire-aligned feline. She hoped it was the former.

Wendy said, "We could maybe be swayed into a pricier place if the unit is really nice ..."

Archibald's keen eyes seemed to light with the challenge of convincing renters to take on a place beyond their means. "Let's start with the two-bedroom."

Deandra scarcely paid attention to the tour of the upstairs apartment. Archibald, thankfully, had gone back into professional mode and didn't offer even a lewd glance during the showing. Wendy asked a slew of questions, helping to maintain the ruse that they were here as prospective renters. Deandra, leash in hand, allowed Havoc to sniff the apartment at leisure, often dipping into other rooms while Wendy and Archibald chatted elsewhere.

What was on Deandra's mind the most was how they were going to gain access to Ingrid's treasure chest while Archibald was with them. It would be much harder to avoid notice in a studio apartment. Even if he didn't have an issue with showing them the inside of the trunk, seeing as it came with the apartment, he'd be more than suspicious if she pulled a strange blue coin out of her pocket and tried to use it as a key.

Wendy had said on the way over, "Don't worry. I've got an idea for a distraction." Any time Deandra asked what the distraction was, Wendy would say something like "We need genuine reactions" or "I don't want you to get so stressed over details that you over-think it."

At the time, Deandra decided to trust her extroverted cousin, but now she was full of regret. There had to be a middle ground between overthinking and being so shocked by Wendy's impromptu revelations that Deandra choked on her own tongue. She most definitely would have vetoed the plan to turn her into a widow—her avian lover torn from this world via a boating mishap. They hadn't known Archibald was an avian, which meant Wendy had come up with the lie on the spot.

It was both impressive and terrifying. Who knew what could come out of her mouth next ...

Twenty minutes later, the group of four headed downstairs to the studio apartment once inhabited by Ingrid Varros. It was, according to both the website and Archibald himself, the only studio apartment currently available, further confirming this was the right unit.

The studio was five hundred square feet. It was furnished with a stove, a fridge, a small dining table with a single mismatched chair, and a twin bed covered in an ancient-looking floral comforter. The treasure chest sat at the foot of the bed and was topped by a wilting houseplant in a ceramic pot.

Archibald finished the bulk of the tour in five minutes flat, as if he were trying to make the studio seem as unappealing as possible —clearly hoping to push them into renting the more expensive two-bedroom. The moment Wendy and Archibald fell silent, Deandra's pocket issued a quick, sharp shriek.

Or, more accurately, the magical coin in her pocket did. Her face heated as three sets of eyes swiveled her way. Havoc's perturbed expression was punctuated by a low growl, his gaze focused on her jeans' front pocket.

"Cell phone," Deandra said. "Alarm. Uh, reminder. For my ... pills."

Wendy, who stood just behind Archibald flapped her arms in a "What the heck kind of lie is *that*?" gesture. Which was rich coming from the woman who had granted her a deceased avian boyfriend!

"Oh," Archibald said with an air of unease. "Are you ... ill?" He gave her another elevator scan, as if he were worried she was contagious.

"Allergies," she said quickly, thinking of the sneezing fit that had befallen Deandra, Wendy, and the receptionist at Corly Land Management in reaction to the herb satchel inside their delivered welcome basket. "My mundane immune system is still acclimating to Axia."

Archibald nodded once. "Mundanes *are* a bit ... fragile."

Deandra bristled once more.

Another scan. "Your tenacity is enticing, I must say." His head cocked sharply to the side as he regarded her, unnervingly birdlike.

She suppressed a shudder.

"I have an inquiry!" Wendy said entirely too loudly and in an unrecognizable accent.

Archibald tore his gaze from Deandra to address Wendy. "Yes?"

"Could you show me the outdoor facilities? The parking lot. The dumpsters. I read there's a nearby laundry facility we can access with a key?"

Nodding, he said, "Of course. We can—"

The traitorous coin shrieked again.

Deandra ineffectually clapped a hand over a pocket that clearly didn't have a cell phone in it. Her other hand—the one with a leash loop wrapped around it—went to her stomach and she moaned pitifully, hoping it drowned out the coin's soft wailing. "Would it be okay if I used the bathroom? The allergy medicine is a pretty high dose and does a number on my stomach." She offered a smile that no doubt showed too many teeth.

The coin vibrated hard under Deandra's palm, startling her so much she shrieked a little herself.

Archibald looked mildly scandalized, clearly concerned this weak-stomached mundane might relieve herself on the floor. "Uh, yes. Of course. We'll be around back. Just turn the lock on the bottom knob and close door behind you when you leave."

Deandra issued another surprised cry when the coin not only vibrated, but heated in her pocket.

Archibald all but grabbed Wendy by the arm before gently guiding her out the door, then closed it behind them. It reopened a second later, and he poked his head in. "Perhaps crack a window when you exit as well." The door closed with a snick.

Deandra was mortified.

She hurried to the apartment door and locked it, which would only buy her a couple of seconds if Wendy couldn't keep Archibald occupied very long, but it would at least give her a few precious moments to bolt into the bathroom.

Letting Havoc's leash go, she darted to the treasure chest and picked up the small potted plant. She placed it in the kitchen sink and turned the faucet on, quickly soaking the dry soil before shutting off the tap and rushing back to the trunk. She pulled the coin out of her pocket as she went.

Glaring at the coin, she whisper-hissed, "I'm hoping you were making all that racket because you recognize the trunk. Key calling to lock?"

The coin didn't react. Which was comforting, honestly. The

idea of a soul or a consciousness being trapped in the metal disc was too disturbing.

The trunk was about five feet long and three feet tall, its rounded lid giving it extra height. The body was made of a deep-brown wood, and a now-familiar bluish metal made up the bands that ran crosswise over the lid and decorated each of the trunk's corners. A circular handle made of coiled metal hung from each end of the trunk.

The outside was smooth, as far as keyholes went—even holes the size and shape of a coin. The two steel latches attached to the front of the lid were easy to flip up, and though padlocks might have once hung from their holes, none did now.

Blowing out a long breath, she braced herself and used both hands to open the trunk's lid, expecting it not to budge. It whispered open on well-oiled hinges. The wood had been so smoothed by weather or time, it almost felt like soft leather. She supposed, though, that the wood might have come from a fae realm tree that possessed properties beyond anything that grew here.

She realized a moment later that she'd slammed one eye shut in apprehension of what might lie inside the trunk—or what might come flying out.

But, as Deandra had originally suspected, the trunk was empty. Her heart sank to her toes—not only for herself, but for Petunia. Deandra had hoped that the trunk would be chock full of Ingrid's tools or rare fae metals, along with an envelope with "For Petunia" scrawled on the front.

Granted, opening the trunk with her mundane strength instead of the coin probably meant that something very valuable *had* once been inside the trunk and had since been removed.

With the lid propped up on the footrest of the bed, Deandra ran her free hand over the edges of the trunk—all four sides, the base, and the underside of the lid. No hidden divots fit for a coin. No traditional keyholes were on the inside either. She'd hoped there might be a little tab to pull on the floor of the trunk, revealing a false bottom. No such luck there either.

Sighing and sitting back on her haunches, she opened her palm to address the coin. "Any ideas, coin?"

Nothing.

Havoc trotted up next to her. Getting on his hind legs, he placed his front paws on the trunk's lip and peered in. After five seconds, he chirped once, snorted, and then wandered off, apparently uninterested.

On a whim, Deandra placed the coin in the bottom of the trunk, then pulled her hand away. She chewed on the inside of her cheek. Maybe the coin would shriek or buzz or hum in distress in reaction to a lack of contact, and that would trigger something inside the trunk.

Still, nothing happened.

Sighing, she was ready to call this endeavor a wash when a bright blue light suddenly blasted out of the trunk. It startled her so badly, she fell onto her backside. Havoc rushed over to make sure she was okay, and somehow that turned into him knocking her flat on her back while he furiously licked her face. She cackled, trying to swat him away.

When she finally broke free, she righted herself and crawled back to the trunk. Havoc crept along next to her. The entire inside of the trunk's once-black lining was now covered in glowing blue runes.

She stared into the trunk, willing it to do something else. When several long seconds ticked by without incident, Havoc propped his front paws on the lip of the trunk and offered it a tentative chirp-bark.

Nothing.

Shrugging, Deandra cautiously reached into the trunk to extract the coin. At this point, she'd done all she could think to do, so now it was a matter of getting the coin into Petunia's possession without raising too much suspicion. Could she place the coin in an envelope and leave it under Petunia's welcome mat, much like Ingrid had? She had no idea where the woman lived.

Deandra's brows slammed together when she attempted to pick up the coin, only to have it stick fast to the trunk's floor. "What the heck?"

Havoc chirped softly.

She tried to wedge her nails under the coin to pry it loose, but it was as if it were superglued in place. She placed three fingertips on the coin's surface and pushed forward, wondering if she could slide it toward the back of the trunk and then use the wall as leverage.

The moment she pressed down on the coin, though, it sank *into* the trunk's floor. Deandra snatched her hand back.

She watched as the coin slowly lowered, the runes around it shifting to make room. Havoc pressed his side against hers; she wasn't sure if he was aware he'd done it. She leaned against him too.

When the coin was flush with the base of the chest, the runes all winked out at once. Havoc chirped in alarm. Deandra gasped. She didn't fall onto her back like an overturned turtle this time, so that was a win.

One second, two—the trunk gave a creak, and the floor of the trunk swung up like a trapdoor, stopping a few inches from being flush with the back.

In the revealed compartment lay a book, thick and leather-bound. She reached in to pull it free, then rested its back on the lip of the trunk. The title was in a language Deandra didn't recognize —or at least she thought she didn't. The words on the cover initially had been as decipherable as gibberish, and then ... *somehow* she understood them.

### The Realm's Most Misunderstood Breed: The Dire Wolf

## A Guide for Ambitious Pet Owners

Seconds before the text changed, Deandra would have said the symbols were runes. After learning that the coin's markings were very likely Dwarvish, and that Ingrid Varros was a dwarf, Deandra's best guess was that the title of the book had originally been written in Dwarvish, too.

When she convinced herself that she hadn't officially lost her marbles, Deandra was reminded of the day she'd found Havoc. He'd originally sounded like a barking dog, but at some point, his barks had morphed into chirps and peeps. One such bark had seemed to change its mind on its way to her ears. Was something similar happening now?

What hadn't changed at all was the stunning art on the cover. It was a bit faded in places, but the image was of a dire wolf prowling through a dense forest, its shaggy dark-gray coat blending into the foliage. Its bright yellow eyes peered out at her, like glowing embers. The artist had somehow portrayed the wolf's calculating intelligence, unwavering confidence, and fierce predatory nature. It was equal parts gorgeous and terrifying.

Havoc pressed his muzzle to the picture and snuffled at it. His big dog-like eyes met hers, his expression somehow pleading, as if he were demanding an explanation. Did he know this was the kind of creature everyone else saw when they looked at him?

It was hard to answer him, though, when she wasn't sure of the question.

So she said the thing she'd been suspicious of since the beginning. She hadn't actually voiced any of her thoughts to Havoc directly, worried he'd go "berserk," much like Sunshine supposedly had. "This trunk was the property of a woman who, I think, was your owner before me." She tapped the wolf image on the book with one finger. "I think this book is from the fae realm, and it's about dire wolves. But now I'm not sure if your owner *knew* you were a dragon or if she also only saw a dire wolf."

Bracing herself, she asked, "Do you know the name Ingrid Varros?"

Havoc went stock-still, his gaze glued to the cover of the thick tome. Slowly, his scales went from honey-yellow to a muddy brown. Thin wisps of white smoke wafted from his nostrils.

Oh dear.

"Buddy?" she asked gently, starting to pull the book toward herself so she could clasp it to her chest. "Havoc, you can't go flamethrower on me, okay? If you do, you could hurt both of us. And maybe Wendy, too. You don't want that, right?"

Havoc was practically vibrating with what she assumed was rage. All at once, he huffed a great plume of smoke out of his nose that smelled vaguely like a campfire. He pushed off from the trunk and went tearing across the studio apartment, growling and kicking his back feet in the air like an agitated bronco trying to unseat his rider. Deandra stood and kept a wary eye on him, now more concerned about his trailing leash getting caught on something. Thankfully, there were no end tables topped by fancy lamps or expensive vases.

She gave him about a minute to work out his ire, casting furtive glances at the door, convinced Archibald would come back at any moment. "You all right?" she asked when he finally stopped thrashing. He turned to stare at her and huffed an exhausted breath out of his nose, white smoke curling from his nostrils like recently blown-out candles.

She took that as a yes. Needing to return the trunk to its previous state, she laid the book on the bed, hoping to keep it out of Havoc's sight. Moving quickly, she lowered the lid of the false bottom. When it clicked softly into place, the coin rose out of it like it was on a miniature elevator. She easily picked it up. Running the back of her fingers along the area where the coin had been, she found no trace of a divot or circular seam.

The glowing blue symbols hadn't returned.

She closed the lid, flipped the latches back into place, and scooped the book off the bed, being mindful to keep the dire wolf art pressed to her chest so Havoc wouldn't be retriggered. She slid the coin back into her pocket.

"We gotta get out of here," she told Havoc, who trotted toward her as she made her way to the door. She scooped the leash loop off the floor and secured it around her wrist. "We're going to book it to the car and hopefully not get caught on the way. I can't exactly hide something as big as this book under my shirt."

Havoc sneezed, then pawed at his nose.

Deandra wasn't sure if that meant anything but took it as confirmation that he was on board with dabbling in this minor bit of theft.

She unlocked the door, turned the tab on the bottom lock, got herself and Havoc outside, and pulled the door closed behind them. She jiggled the knob to make sure it was locked, then Deandra and her dragon dashed across the parking lot, stolen book tucked close to Deandra's side.

Minutes after Deandra sent Wendy an "All clear!" text, Deandra heard footsteps. She peeked over the hood of Wendy's car, temporarily leaving her hiding place—crouched by the wheel well. Havoc had been chewing fastidiously on one of his back feet, and Deandra's sudden movement startled him so much that he jumped to attention—only to trip over the leash and crash to the ground chin first. He was back on his feet a moment later. He peeped once to let her know he was okay, then gave a full-body shake, like a dog after a bath.

He was an absolutely atrocious guard dragon. She affectionately scratched him under the chin, which appeared to have survived its sudden collision with the asphalt.

By the time Deandra glanced away from her clumsy dragon and back over the hood, Wendy was already rounding the front of the car.

Wendy dropped to a squat in front of her, peered over the hood, then crouched lower. "What the heck are you doing? What are you holding?"

"I didn't know where to hide! You have the car keys!" Deandra whispered back.

The faint snatches of someone singing sounded in the distance.

"Ahh! That's Archibald," Wendy whisper-hissed, eyes wide. "He was singing under his breath a lot while I was trying to kill time in the laundry room. He was obviously getting antsy waiting for me. I must say, he's got the voice of an angel. Stupid avians and their stupid natural ability to sing. I was really stretching for ways to keep him distracted. At one point I was Foraging the washing machine manufacturer's website to look up things like water capacity and drum size!"

It took Deandra a moment to remember that Forage was the hub system's most popular search engine.

The singing grew louder.

"Quick," Wendy said. "Get in the back."

Feeling especially foolish, Deandra stayed hunched over while Wendy hit the button on her key fob. As soon as the locks disengaged, Deandra pulled open the back driver's-side door, then dove in after Havoc. Wendy was already backing out of the parking spot before Deandra had fully closed the door. Havoc clearly thought having a passenger in the back seat with him—especially one flopped over on the seat—was great fun, and he wasted no time pouncing on her head to lightly chew on her ears and lick her face.

"You'll never catch us, coppers!" Wendy crowed triumphantly as she sped out of the lot and took a left onto McClaren Way with more speed than necessary. Deandra was nearly pitched off the seat. Havoc chirped in protest, doing his best to remain on all fours, looking for all the world like a surfer trying to stay atop his board.

Deandra eventually managed to extricate herself from her dragon, who was as hopped up on the thrill of escape as Wendy. "Slow down," she said, laughing. "I don't think Archibald is chasing us."

"We won't know for at least three blocks whether we've lost the tail," Wendy said in a terrible Boston accent. "*Stay* ready so you don't have to *get* ready, as I always say."

Deandra could confirm that Wendy had never said that before today. "Did you have a hard time getting away from Archibald or something? Do we *actually* need to worry about him following us?"

"Nah," Wendy said. "I told him that we'd be in touch soon but that I had to get back to you to make sure your stomach problems weren't too serious. His face screwed up and then he shooed me away. He made a comment about needing to check on the studio apartment to make sure everything was ...*unsoiled.*"

"He did *not* use that word," Deandra said, her face heating in embarrassment, even though her stomach issues had been fabricated.

"He definitely did," Wendy said, then took another entirely too fast turn.

Her getaway-driver dreams were dashed less than a minute later, though, when she had to stop at a stop sign and allow a trio of moms pushing strollers to cross the road. Actually, the last stroller appeared to be occupied by a small Komodo dragon wearing a frilly bonnet.

Deandra shook her head. Nope. That one was too weird. She wasn't going to ask.

It wasn't until she, Wendy, and Havoc were back in Wendy's apartment that Deandra explained what had happened with the coin, the trunk, and the book. The book in question was lying in the middle of the dining room table, the dire wolf image facing Wendy.

Wendy had yet to touch it.

Deandra finished her tale with the thought that had been nagging at her ever since she found the book. "If we can believe everything Petunia said ... Ingrid left the coin and trunk for her. I assume Ingrid took everything but the book because she was in too much of a hurry to take it with her. The book is about dire wolves—just like Havoc's glamour—and how to care for them as a pet. I—"

Wendy held up a hand. "How do you know it's about pet ownership? And since when do you read Dwarvish or runes or whatever this is?"

Deandra looked from Wendy to the book and back again. "The words didn't change to English for you?"

Wendy cocked a brow. "And you say *my* weird detector is broken ..." She held up a hand again to stop Deandra. "Don't spiral yet. Finish what you were saying."

It took a moment for Deandra to get her thoughts back in order. "Ingrid was seen in town the day before the fire—probably when she left Havoc in the dumpster. What if it's not just the book that Ingrid left for her? What if Ingrid wanted Petunia to take care of Havoc—either permanently or until she got back to Axia to pick him up?"

Havoc was asleep under the table, the soft rumble of his snores vibrating Deandra's toes.

"Oh jeez," Wendy said, sounding forlorn. "I didn't even consider that."

Deandra knew the biggest part of her reluctance to tell Petunia about any of this was because she didn't want to lose Havoc. He'd *chosen* Deandra, after all. And he'd gone as berserk as Sunshine had at the mere mention of Ingrid Varros's name. Deandra had to take Havoc's well-being into consideration.

Given how volatile and high-strung Petunia was, Deandra had serious doubts about the woman's ability to take on the responsibility of caring for a dire wolf *or* a dragon. Especially when, by Petunia's own admission, she was willing to give up Ingrid's secrets out of spite. What if Havoc, while in Petunia's care, lost his collar, or Petunia took it off? Would Petunia give up *his* secrets? Would she reveal the realm's first thought-to-be-extinct dragon for her fifteen minutes of fame, in hopes that if she got her *deserved* time in the spotlight, she'd gain a level of notoriety similar to Ingrid Varros's, her hero and nemesis?

Deandra mentally shook her head. No. Until she felt confident Petunia would be willing to put Havoc's needs above her own, Deandra was keeping him, and Petunia wouldn't know he existed. End of story.

Instead of pummeling Deandra with questions, Wendy had pulled the book toward herself and was thumbing through it. It appeared that she'd started somewhere in the middle, letting the thick book flop open in front of her. The book still hadn't switched to English for her, so she was only looking at the pictures. From Deandra's position across the table, she could tell that several of the pages in the section Wendy studied dealt with dire wolf magic types. The book was open to an image depicting a wolf with fur made of flames.

After a minute or two, Wendy glanced up. "You okay?"

Deandra shrugged. "I don't really know what to do now."

Wendy nodded and flipped the book closed. She ran her fingers over the leather cover, skirting the image of the wolf, mindful that too much direct handling might cause the image to flake off even more. "I wonder if this is a standard fae realm book or it's a special edition." She lifted the front cover, briefly admiring the small metal pieces that decorated the corners, much like the corners of the treasure chest. "Oh!" she said, and let the cover fall all the way open, the metal corners clicking softly against the table.

Deandra saw it before Wendy picked it up.

A folded slip of paper lay against the book's title page, "Petunia" written in a looping scrawl.

Wendy held the folded slip between two fingers and waved it. "There's no envelope. We can easily say it fell out of the book, and we didn't realize who it was for until after we read it. It's not like it was in a sealed envelope and we steamed it open ..."

Deandra chewed on the inside of her cheek. "You have to stop reading if it's really personal or something."

But Wendy was already unfolding the letter. "*Hello, Petunia,*" she read. Then Wendy stilled. "Whoa."

"What?" Deandra asked, leaning forward.

"The words just vanished." Wendy flipped the page over, as if the words had all scurried off one side of the page and onto the other. Not even Petunia's name was written on the sheet anymore.

"Can I see it?" Deandra asked.

Shrugging, Wendy handed it over.

The moment Deandra's fingertips touched the page, words etched themselves across the cream-colored parchment. Startled, she dropped it. Before her eyes, the words vanished again. "What the heck ..." she whispered to herself.

Havoc, upon hearing the fuss, woke with a snort. He poked his head between her knees and rested his chin on her thigh. Laughing softly, she scooted back in her chair so she could properly give him a scritch behind the ears. "I'm okay," she said, somehow knowing that was concern in his big, puppy-dog eyes.

He peeped once, then scrambled very ungracefully onto the chair beside her. Wendy didn't love the idea of a dog sitting at the dining room table, but she and Havoc had called a truce; he was allowed to sit there as long as he kept his paws off the table. Deandra noted, as she often did, that Wendy's eyeline when she looked at Havoc was always at some spot *above* his head, since she saw him as a dire wolf unless his ever-present collar was off.

"No paws," Wendy reminded him.

Havoc chirped once.

Blowing out a slow breath, Deandra returned her focus to what she now assumed was a magicked piece of paper—a magicked piece of paper that had been inside a magicked book. She cautiously picked the note up again. Havoc woofed softly when apparently he, too, saw the words reappear.

"*Hello, stranger*," the first line now read.

Despite that being creepy as all get-out, Deandra might have suffered heart failure if the note had somehow known her name. She tested reading the note out loud, wondering if this was a "for the reader's eyes only" kind of spell, but after she read the first line out loud to Wendy, the words stayed in place.

"I feel strangely left out," Wendy said, pouting dramatically.

"I feel entirely *freaked* out, if that helps," Deandra said.

"A little. Keep reading."

Deandra cleared her throat and read.

*Hello, stranger. Color me impressed, as this spell can only be triggered by someone who's gained the dragon's trust. Not even I can claim that honor. When he's glamoured, he doesn't show me his true self. He's been glamoured since he was only a few months old. I frankly didn't think Petunia would be capable of it either, and had I not severed so many connections and burned so many bridges, I never would have turned to Petunia for help. Desperate times call for desperate measures and all that.*

*Anyway, as you must have no doubt figured out yourself, this book is about the dragon's cover story to help you better understand the breed the dragon is unknowingly pretending to be. It will switch to English for anyone on the spell's approved list—myself, Petunia, and … you.*

*A dire wolf's behavior is <u>very</u> different from that of a dragon—especially a Ruber clan dragon—so this is to help you understand the reactions you may get if people see you with the dog. This could be quite the challenge, as the dragon trusts you, and dragons from the Ruber clan are the most loyal of dragonkind.*

Havoc chirped, his chest puffed up like a proud peacock. Wendy and Deandra both laughed. Pleased with himself, Havoc let his tongue loll out the side of his mouth.

*Without going into detail that could incriminate you if you're later questioned, just know that I happened upon an egg many months ago that then hatched. The egg had been in the possession of an individual who had acquired it under even more dubious circumstances than I had, and I liberated the egg to protect the precious cargo inside.*

*My decisions, to put it lightly, have caught up with me. If you've already gained the dragon's trust, I'm confident you'll keep him safe until I return. It's imperative that no one learns of who he really is. It's not only his life that would be threatened if the truth about him is revealed, but that of this entire town—hells, possibly the hub system itself. Never forget that it's not only his secret to keep.*

*There are some who would stop at nothing to*

acquire him, and I assure you many—if not most—would not act in the dragon's best interests.

I don't know how you got the coin from Petunia or gained access to the heirloom trunk. It doesn't matter. You being admitted into the dragon's pod overrides everything else. I know he will be safe with you, stranger. I thank you for caring for him when I cannot.

I have a few failsafes in place in case the trouble that chases me is able to catch me. If that comes to pass, someone will come to Axia to fetch the dragon for me. They have been given permission to use whatever means necessary to do so. Do not resist. I have grand plans for him, and those plans will not only change his life, but mine. He and I will change the world.

He is not yours. Remember that.

Enjoy your time with him now—you've been granted an opportunity not even many in the fae realm could dream to experience.

Be vigilant,
Ingrid Varros

Deandra stared at the note for a long time, dumbfounded, before dropping it to the table. As the paper fluttered to the surface, the words vanished.

Havoc nuzzled his head under her elbow and peered up at her, her arm draped over his head like a visor. He peeped softly. Deandra's throat tightened and tears pricked her eyes.

"*He is not yours. He is not yours. He is not yours,*" repeated in her head like a mantra.

She'd known that, of course. He'd been well taken care of until he'd been dumped ... hidden ... whatever Ingrid wanted to label it. Something catastrophic had clearly happened for Ingrid to abandon Havoc—even temporarily. But he'd been abandoned all the same.

Most of what Deandra knew of Ingrid was through the lens of Petunia, who was admittedly biased against the dwarf. Maybe she wasn't as awful as Petunia implied, but there must have been at least some truth in what she said. Given how attached to Havoc Deandra had become, the idea of turning him over to Ingrid made her stomach twist.

"*I have grand plans for him, and those plans will not only change his life, but mine. He and I will change the world,*" the note had said.

It sounded like Havoc was just a commodity to Ingrid—not a pet, not a companion. Ingrid's note didn't speak of their bond, or how much she'd miss him. She hadn't mentioned a name or favorite foods. Havoc hadn't looped Ingrid into his pod, even after she'd raised him from a hatchling. Heck, when he'd heard her name, he'd gone postal.

Didn't Havoc get any say in his own future, even if he didn't have the ability to voice those wants?

Out of the corner of her eye, she saw Wendy reach for the note once more, clearly unable to resist further examining a magical object. She and Heather were similar in that way.

"Oh," Wendy said, staring down at the letter. Her eyes frantically scanned the page, as if she were worried the presumably newly formed words would vanish on her again if she didn't read them fast enough. "The note is back to how it was earlier. And the words seem to be sticking around this time. I'm guessing the magic woven into the paper is diminished now, if not outright depleted, after the secret note revealed itself to you ..."

Deandra reached for the paper, and Wendy handed it over. Wendy appeared to be right: The words didn't vanish or shift anymore. Huh. She handed the note back, still a little creeped out by the whole thing.

Wendy accepted it and scanned the page. "Let's see ... the part about the egg being acquired by vaguely criminal means? Now it says it's a dire wolf puppy, and that the collar it's wearing is for behavioral control. She says if it's ever removed, the wolf will tear Petunia's limbs from her torso." Wendy winced as her gaze skated over a few more lines. "Jeez, this lady should write horror. I'm not going to read that last part to you. It says the puppy's secret needs to be kept at all costs, and then she lists the addresses of Petunia's parents and her siblings. There's yet another very elaborately detailed threat about the various things that can happen if she tells the dire wolf's secrets to anyone. From what I could tell from the book's pictures, there are several chapters about how dangerous the breed is in the wrong hands. The puppy section is at least five chapters long. No wonder people freak out so bad about the breed —and why Ranger Vicks—"

Havoc growled.

"And why *the bad man*," Wendy amended, "was so determined to get Havoc off the streets."

Deandra supposed that could be an explanation as to why Ingrid had chosen such a maligned breed of dog to be Havoc's glamour. She probably hadn't accounted for the likes of Ranger Vicks, though. If Petunia had been in possession of Havoc when that altercation with the rangers had gone down, Havoc would still be in Parks Management custody. Deandra was sure of it. Who knew where he'd be now, or who would have learned his identity.

Wendy awkwardly cleared her throat. When she had Deandra's attention, her gaze flicked to Havoc for a moment before gently asking, "You're not actually thinking of giving him up to Petunia, are you?"

Before Deandra could say, "No, of course not," Havoc let out a soft plaintive howl, the likes of which Deandra hadn't heard since day one, when he'd dramatically let his hunger be known. When she glanced down at him, his big sad eyes almost did her in.

"Never," she told him, even if she wasn't sure that was a promise she could keep.

Havoc peeped and lunged toward her. With his back legs on the chair, and his front paws on her shoulders, he furiously licked her nose. She laughed and gently batted him away. Once he was back in his chair, she glanced at her cousin, finding her watching them with a small smile and teary eyes.

"You two are a team, no matter what some mean dwarf lady says," Wendy said. "We can't know who's coming for Havoc or when, but I'll help make sure you *stay* a team, okay?"

Deandra teared up, too. She wasn't even sure why. Maybe it was just nice to be reminded you had people in your corner. "Thanks, Wendy."

Havoc threw his head back and attempted something approximating a celebratory roar—though he sounded a bit like kid's toy afflicted with dying batteries. Deandra wondered what full-grown dragons from the Ruber clan sounded like when they roared. She pictured a massive Havoc towering over her—but with the same exuberance as the giant red puppy from one of her favorite kid's books. Would he eventually be so huge that he towered over houses?

She gave her head a shake. She'd live in the moment with Havoc as much as she could.

As his warbling roar subsided, he grinned at her, tongue lolling, clearly delighted with himself. She grinned back.

For the second time in a matter of weeks, Deandra found herself peering into a plant, hoping the current resident was home. This time, she was looking for a homicidal fire newt rather than a clan of pixies, though. She and Wendy had gone over their plan ad nauseam last night, but now that she was here, her nerves were kicking into high gear.

"Sunshine?" she asked, hands on her knees. "Can we talk? I

think I figured out what you were trying to tell me. The coin you gave me belonged to ..." She braced herself. "Ingrid Varros?"

A few breaths passed in silence.

And then a screeching fire newt was streaking toward her from the depths of the shrub like a possessed flying squirrel. Deandra's reflexes kicked into overdrive, and her hand shot up just in time to catch the crazed amphibian around her middle before she latched onto Deandra's face.

*Hiss!*

"Oh, calm down!" Deandra said, exasperated, her heart racing. She gave Sunshine a gentle shake for good measure.

She held the newt in her fist as she would a burrito—a clammy, *wiggly* burrito. Sunshine's two front feet rested on Deandra's thumb, and she cocked her head to better look at Deandra with one beady eye.

Wendy and Havoc stood somewhere behind her. The dragon was making small, distressed noises, probably because he didn't trust Sunshine any more than Deandra did. She hoped Wendy had a good hold on Havoc's leash.

"I need you to listen to me," she told the newt. "Hiss once for yes, twice for no, okay?"

*Hiss!*

Deandra issued an internal cheer; she hadn't been sure if Sunshine understood her well enough for this method of communication to work.

"Before you ended up in a terrarium in Mythic Pet Kitchen, you were a pet of Ingrid Varros, right?"

Sunshine's yellow spots went from pastel yellow to neon in a matter of seconds. Her little body warmed in Deandra's hand at an alarming rate and it took everything in Deandra's power not to fling the newt back into the bushes.

Sunshine's body cooled a few seconds later. *Hiss.*

"Did you know Ingrid was in Axia?"

Long pause. *Hiss, hiss.*

Had Sunshine only just now gotten confirmation that Ingrid had been in town? Perhaps the newt *had* seen her, though, and didn't know it, given Ingrid's many disguises. Sunshine's reason for giving Deandra the coin could have been that; the newt had wanted to know if her former owner had been here or if the coin had ended up in town by some other means.

Deandra asked, "Were you with her when she decided to go into hiding?"

*Hiss!*

"Did she take you with her?"

*Hiss, hiss.*

Deandra considered that for a moment. Sunshine had been part of Ingrid's menagerie when Ingrid pulled up stakes on her life, but she'd left Sunshine behind. "Was Havoc—the dire wolf behind me—with you and Ingrid, too, when she went into hiding?"

Sunshine cocked her head curiously. Somehow, Deandra got the impression that the newt wasn't confused by the question so much as she didn't know the answer. Her eyes darted around a bit as she worked through something. Then she suddenly wiggled and flailed in Deandra's grasp.

Deandra's panic that the newt had snapped and was planning her demise was short-lived. It was soon clear that Sunshine wasn't attempting homicide, nor was she trying to escape. She twisted herself in Deandra's hand until she was holding onto Deandra's middle finger and had wedged her snout between that finger and the pointer finger. Her back now faced Deandra.

Turning her wrist at an awkward angle so she could see the newt better, Deandra watched, bewildered, as Sunshine tried acting something out. With her front feet holding onto the length of Deandra's middle finger, she shook it back and forth. At one point, the newt made a fist and pounded it gently on Deandra's pointer finger. She hissed and shook and raged as if she were—

"Oh! You were usually caged when you were with Ingrid? So Havoc *might* have been there, but you were kept separate?"

Sunshine hissed once, then quickly turned around in Deandra's hand so she was positioned facing her again, with her front feet on her thumb and her back feet propped on her pinky. The newt hissed again.

How had Sunshine ended up in Axia, then? Sunshine had said she hadn't known Ingrid was in town.

"Did she ... sell you before she left her previous home?" Deandra ventured.

*Hiss.*

Deandra couldn't tell how Sunshine felt about that. Had Sunshine gone berserk at the sound of Ingrid's name because she detested the dwarf with the same passion Havoc apparently did, or was Sunshine upset about being not only abandoned but sold off?

"Maybe part of why she came to Axia was because she was looking for you," Deandra said.

Sunshine didn't have eyebrows to raise dubiously, but her expression suggested it all the same. *Hiss, hiss.*

"I'm sorry she sold you," Deandra said. "And I'm sorry you ended up with someone just as bad, if not worse."

*Hiss,* Sunshine said, head lowered. Somehow she sounded both crestfallen *and* resigned.

"Ingrid is gone now, as far as I know," Deandra said. "I think you're safe to live in the park, if that's what you want." Reluctantly, she added, "Unless you wanted *me* to adopt—"

*Hiss, hiss!*

"Not nice," Deandra muttered, even though she was relieved Sunshine didn't want to be adopted any more than Deandra wanted to do the adopting. "Think you can stay out of trouble here? No more tormenting park visitors?"

Sunshine's hesitation was a bit too long for comfort. *Hiss!*

"Then let's make a deal—if you keep your promise not to harass anyone, I won't tell Parks Management about any of this. And let's also promise that if we ever see Ingrid in town, we'll warn the other, okay? She abandoned my friend back there, and I think she might come back for him one day."

Sunshine scrambled out of Deandra's hand, quick as a snake, and was on her shoulder a breath later. Deandra froze, arm still held up in front of her, very aware of the unpredictable fire newt mere inches from her ear. The newt was presumably sizing up Wendy and Havoc behind her.

A blink later, and Sunshine was perched on Deandra's forearm. A tense moment passed as the newt stared at Deandra intensely with one eye. With a sudden quick nod, Sunshine turned and dove for the bush, disappearing inside with only a slight rustle of leaves.

Deandra turned to Wendy and Havoc and gave a full-body shudder, shaking out her arms. As she walked toward them, Wendy let the leash go, and Havoc bounded over, prancing around Deandra's feet and chirping excitedly.

"Negotiation complete?" Wendy asked when Deandra reached her.

"I ... think so?" Deandra said, then scooped the leash loop off the ground. "Hard to tell with homicidal fire newts, you know?"

Wendy peered around her. "Uh. So is the fact that the shrub now has gray smoke pooling underneath it a good thing or a bad thing?" She straightened and stared at Deandra wide-eyed.

Deandra's eyes widened, too. "We should go."

They hurried out of the park without looking back.

THE FOLLOWING EVENING, Deandra and Wendy were crouched in strategic hiding places in the parking lot of In Flux We Trust. Deandra was behind a large rectangular planter holding an orange tree, and Wendy was squatting around the corner of the mechanic shop. They each periodically peeked out from their spots to check the activity—or lack thereof—in the lot. The latest black-smithing class would be ending soon ... especially since, according to the website's sign-up list, no one had registered. Deandra wondered how Glenn was faring with the interviews for Petunia's replacement.

"Oh! There she is!" Wendy whispered, then pulled back so she was shielded by the corner of the shop.

Deandra hunkered a little lower behind her potted tree. After a few seconds, she poked her head out and got visual confirmation that Petunia had picked up the envelope they'd left in her bicycle's front basket. Deandra quickly ducked low when Petunia sharply turned around, clearly scanning the parking lot for the person who had delivered the gift. Inside the envelope was the coin and a note.

Deandra had penned the note herself.

Dear Ms. Hartley,

We know of your association with Ms. Varros. We also know you lost the coin. While we considered keeping it, it's not what Ms. Varros wanted. She trusted you, so we will, too. We would have returned it sooner but decided to restore it to its former glory first.

We can confirm that the treasure chest Ms. Varros left behind is empty. Do not fret. The real treasure is the coin itself. It's forged from magic-infused gold from the fae realm —a trinket most rare!

You could sell it on a Forage site for a sizable sum. That's your right.

But may we present an alternative?

Consider making a donation to a fae-realm-focused museum. You'd no doubt be recognized handsomely for your generosity—not to mention the contribution you'd be making to dwarven youth for years to come, ensuring they don't lose hold of their heritage. Understanding one's history leads to an appreciation of the present, does it not?

The choice, however, is yours.
We know Ms. Varros chose well.

Deandra felt a little bad about keeping Petunia in the dark about Havoc, but she couldn't risk telling his secrets to anyone she didn't fully trust. On that, she and Ingrid Varros were in agreement. The coin, though, she was happy to give to Petunia. The coin was something Ingrid had *wanted* to gift to the woman. Havoc, however, was a different story. Even though Ingrid had planned—in desperation—to hand over his well-being to Petunia, she hadn't been willing to tell Petunia the truth about him. She hadn't believed Havoc would trust her enough to let her into his pod, either.

"I think she's okay with this," Wendy whispered.

Deandra poked her head above the lip of the planter. Petunia held the envelope to her chest and was twirling in a circle outside the shop.

The small smile that graced Deandra's face slipped off as her mind scampered down a rabbit trail. What if Petunia sold the coin, turned the money over to the glamourer she'd found on the arcane web, and then used her newly purchased glamouring talisman to assume Ingrid's likeness before committing literal identity theft? Had they just supplied the funding for a villain origin story?

Wendy and Deandra scrambled to stay hidden when Petunia eventually hopped on her bike, heading out of the parking lot and toward their hiding spots. Petunia was on the phone from the sound of it, though, and she was so caught up in her current circumstances that she didn't even glance their way. Deandra spotted the white sliver of an earbud in the woman's ear, her wild mop of hair pulled into a ponytail that fluttered behind her as she rode.

"Yes, the Power Smash 9000—is it still available? Glenn Walker from In Flux We Trust in Axia called about it a few weeks ago. I'm placing the order on his behalf. I'll be flush with cash *very* soon ..."

When Petunia was out of sight, Wendy and Deandra got to their feet. And not a second too soon; one of Deandra's hamstrings had started to seize up.

Wendy expelled an exaggerated sigh of relief. "Thank the Goddess she's planning to use the money to buy a power hammer and not to hire a gang of pixienappers."

"You thought she was going to the dark side, too?" Deandra asked.

"Oh, one hundred percent," Wendy said. "We made the right call."

Deandra hoped her cousin was right.

Wendy had parked around the block to help ensure Petunia didn't see them arrive.

The car ride home was short and quiet, Deandra lost in her thoughts.

They'd only been in the apartment for three seconds before Havoc was bounding over to them. He tripped on a pair of Deandra's shoes she'd left by the door, and he managed a rather impressive barrel roll that had him flipping head over tail before landing at her feet on his back. His tongue hung out the side of his mouth, and he panted heavily. He looked a touch mad from this angle. Deandra laughed and squatted to give his belly a scratch.

He scrambled to his feet, jumped up to give her nose a drive-by lick, and then darted into the kitchen. He chirped and bounced in several circles before he dramatically plopped onto his haunches, threw his head back and howled.

After they'd all eaten dinner, they settled on the couch to watch a movie. Havoc lay sprawled across their laps, with his back feet and tail draped over Wendy's lap and his head on Deandra's thigh. The dragon snored softly.

Her guilt ebbed away.

Havoc *was* hers, no matter what Ingrid said. If someone came for him, Deandra would fight to keep him. Wendy would, too.

For now, they were together.
And that was all that mattered.

animal charges and poaching clients from Sarah to making false claims about possessing "zoolingual" abilities. The sticking point is Lydia's questionable acquisition of a lucrative gig offered by Oleander Basnet, a yeti whose son needs one-on-one care. Sarah's company fought hard for the opportunity, only to have yet another job snatched away by Lydia.

The peaceful get-together is interrupted when a late arrival informs the group that Lydia has been found murdered. Worse still, the time of death doesn't exonerate anyone at the event. Dee fears she's just shared discounted appetizers with a murderer.

Later that night, a job offer from Oleander hits Dee's inbox. Dee's wallet desperately wants her to take the job, but could there be someone in town so desperate to beat the competition that they murdered Lydia? And could Dee be next?

Find out at https://melissajacksonbooks.com/series/a-mythical-case-of-arson

While waiting for the next book in the Mythical Pet Sitting Mystery series, you can check out the Witch of Edgehill series. There are five books—and the series is complete! (They're all in audio, too!)

Book 1 is *Pawsitively Poisonous.*

*Every town has its secrets, but no one has a secret like hers.*

Amber Blackwood, lifelong resident of Edgehill, Oregon, has earned a reputation for being a semi-reclusive odd duck. Her store, The Quirky Whisker, is full of curiosities, from extremely potent sleepy teas and ever-burning candles to kids' toys that seem to run endlessly without the aid of batteries. The people of Edgehill think of the Quirky Whisker as an integral part of their feline-obsessed town, but most give Amber herself a wide berth. Amber prefers it that way; it keeps her secret safe. But that secret is thrown into jeopardy when Amber's friend Melanie is found dead, a vial of headache tonic from Amber's store clutched in her hand.

Edgehill's newest police chief has had it out for Amber since he arrived three years before. He can't possibly know she's a witch, but his suspicions about her odd store and even odder behavior have shot her to the top of his suspect list. When the Edgehill rumor mill finds out Melanie was poisoned, it's not only the police chief who looks at Amber differently. Determined to both find justice for her friend and to clear her own name, Amber must use her unique gifts to help track down Melanie's real killer. A quest that threatens much more than her secret …

Get it right meow at https://melissajacksonbooks.com/witch-of-edgehill-mysteries/pawsitively-poisonous

# ABOUT THE AUTHOR

Melissa has had a love of stories for as long as she can remember, but only started penning her own during her freshman year of college. She majored in Wildlife, Fish, and Conservation Biology at UC Davis. Yet, while she was neck-deep in organic chemistry and physics, she kept finding herself writing stories in the back of the classroom about fairies and trolls and magic. She finished her degree, but it never captured her heart the way writing did.

Now she owns her own dog walking business (that's sort of wildlife related, right?) by day ... and afternoon and night ... and writes whenever she gets a spare moment. She alternates mostly between fantasy and mystery (often with a paranormal twist). All her books have some element of "other" to them ... witches, ghosts, UFOs. There's no better way to escape the real world than getting lost in a fictional one.

She lives in Northern California with her very patient boyfriend and way too many pets.

You can find out more about her upcoming books and join her newsletter at: https://melissajacksonbooks.com